THE THING ABOUT LOVE...©

A NOVEL BY

J M RAPHAELLE

J M Raphaelle

JMad's House Publishing
Instagram: JMRaphaelle
Twitter: J_M_Raphaelle
FB: JMRaphaelleAuthor & AuthorJMR
www.JMRaphaelle.com

J M Raphaelle

THE THING ABOUT LOVE...

"Jack,"

Thank you for the memories...

J M Raphaelle

Mom,
I love you and miss you, always!

"Marie,"
It was a hell of a ride!

"Rob,"
You're a "once in a lifetime" kind of guy...

To Pao, Miri and Kris,
Thank you for your friendship, support, and shenanigans, which are
exemplified by the "Marie" of this tale...

To the family and friends who kindly took the time to read
— partially or completely — one of the many versions
of this manuscript...
To Sandy, the patience you had every time I got stuck
and had a question about the Spanish translation
is a virtue few possess.

Thank you!

J M Raphaelle

CHAPTER 1

"**P**lease get up, Ellie. You haven't eaten since yesterday morning, and you're starting to worry me."

Marie is standing next to my bed with a tray of food, pleading with me to get up and face life.

"I'm declaring your weekend pity-party done!"

"I really don't want to," I moan into my pillow.

"Okay, but at least eat. Please. I don't want to have to call your mom to tell her you're starving yourself, and I've had to hospitalize you," she insists.

"It's not that bad," I argue.

But it is.

It's been five months, five long months of feeling empty and tattered.

Ever since the darkness and cold settled inside

me.

Ever since the sun stopped rising for me, and all the warmth left my body.

Five months since he left me. My love left me, and I don't know why.

My head is aching. I should probably eat.

Marie continues standing over me, looming, willing me to come to my senses.

"Ellie Isabel Valencia, please get up!"

Marie Sofia Alba has been my best friend since kindergarten. We grew up together in Chicago, until her dad was offered a job in Los Angeles that he couldn't turn down, and they moved to the City of Angels at the end of eighth grade. The distance brought us closer. We've been there for each other through all the major milestones and all the trivial occasions of our lives. She's the only one who can push me beyond my comfort limits and, in this case, my unreasonable self.

I sit up slowly, more for her sake than mine. It's not easy to ruffle Marie, but the compassion reflecting in her eyes shows just how worried she is. She's powerless to help me, and it's getting to her. I don't want to be responsible for her distress. I have a hard enough time coping with my own.

"Okay, I'm up," I mope and cross my legs.

She sighs with relief, "Some days you seem to be doing so much better, but then..."

"I know," I interrupt. "But when night falls and

all is quiet, my thoughts begin to wander and get the best of me. I'll try to do better, I promise."

"It's been five months, Ellie, five months. You're seriously going to stay in bed every weekend, wearing those old PJs, not eating, and hiding from the world?" she reprimands.

As upset as I'm making her, she's gone all out, hoping I'll eat, and prepared a hearty meal for me: scrambled eggs, bacon, toast, fresh fruit, and tea.

She doesn't understand the depth of the agony I'm going through. I don't blame her. Half the time, I don't understand it either.

My irrational self is having a duel-to-the-death with my rational self, and irrational is winning.

I'm broken hearted, and I insist on dwelling in the pain. In part because it ended so abruptly — he didn't even bother to actually break up with me, he just disappeared. And if I'm really being honest, I deceived myself into thinking the relationship was actually real. I feel foolish and duped...duped by my own feeble heart.

"Thank you," I hug her, then take the tea from the tray she's placed on my bed and reach for the toast. I finish it and grab the fruit. The rest is too much. "That's all I can handle right now," I say in a sorrowful tone.

"Okay, but get up, take a shower, and let's go out and get some fresh air," she begs.

I twist my mouth, not keen on the idea, but she

ignores my discontent.

"Enough is enough, Ellie! I know you love him, but I have to be honest, he might have just done you a favor."

I scowl at her, but she doesn't stop.

"I've known the guy since I arrived in LA and consider him a friend, but he's not exactly Prince Charming."

Way to rub it in!

I roll my eyes, clearly showing my displeasure at her tough-love approach, but she continues.

"I'm just saying maybe he's not prepared to love you the way you should be loved, or need to be loved. And by leaving you, he's giving you the opportunity to find a great guy who will."

Whatever, I love him and that's that!

Nothing she's saying is registering in my current reality, true as it may be. The fact is that I don't want to hear it.

"Where's the smart Ellie I know? You're better than this poor, withering little girl," she scolds. "Please listen to me, Ellie, or I'll call Rob, and maybe he'll give you a swift kick in the ass," she adds frustrated.

My bestie in New York? No, he'll talk my ear off!

I roll my eyes again feeling chastised. I scoot out of bed, grab my iPhone, and drag myself to the bathroom without saying another word.

As much as her words sting, I have to admit she's right, but right now I just can't process it.

Maybe a shower will help, or at least get me out of earshot of Marie's "sensible" advice, which I'm stubbornly choosing to ignore.

I turn on the shower, put on some music, and peel off the old, pink PJs that need a good wash. I lean my hands against the vanity and get a quick peek in the mirror, while Luz Casal's lovely voice sings, "Piensa en Mí."

I've created a personalized commiseration playlist that includes No Doubt's "Don't Speak," Adele's "Don't You Remember," Christina Perri's "Jar of Hearts," Shakira's "No," and Billy Vera's "At This Moment," among other heartbreak songs. I've gone there. I *am* there! And it's on auto replay.

Ugh, the reflection in the mirror staring back is pathetic: big brown eyes, dark circles, pale like a ghost, blotched red nose, raven hair in disarray, and gaunt — I've lost at least 15 lbs. since he left me.

How can I be this broken at 22 years old? A girl that once had so many plans, so many life expectations is now undone.

Marie is right, I have to help myself, but how?

The shower's warm water falling over me hides the unwelcome tears rolling down my cheeks. I bring my hands to my face in a pitiful attempt to suppress my sobs. I've shed so many tears, I should've run out already.

I thought time healed all wounds. I'm still waiting...

Has it really been five months? What did I do wrong? How could I have misread our relationship so badly? Why did I believe he loved me when he really didn't? Why didn't I see the signs?

I'm asking the same questions I've been asking myself every day for the past five months. The same wretched questions that have caused my life to spiral out of control.

If he had only told me why he left...

In the solitude of the shower, I think back to that day when I forced him to speak to me. I go over every detail of our non-breakup breakup, and his involuntary explanation, in search of the answers he never gave me.

CHAPTER 2

FOUR MONTHS AGO

Sam is taking Marie to his friend's wedding. He's into her, but she won't go out without me — she's concerned about my post-break up isolation, so she drags me along everywhere.

I'm actually in mild spirits, enough to manage a few forced smiles and some small talk at the wedding reception. But it doesn't take long before I spot him, Mike Aragon, the guy responsible for my month-long broken heart. He's cheerfully chatting with Jack and Mario.

Mike Aragon, Sam Galeas, Jack Milian, and Mario Mesa have been best friends since they were kids. They obviously have the same friends in common, so of course Mike's here.

The three amigos are standing close to the

stage where the band is set up. Marie and I follow Sam to meet them. I feel an ache of nervousness in the pit of my stomach as I start walking toward them, looking down at my feet.

This is the first time I'll be seeing him since the day he left me a month ago. The first time I'll be speaking to him, because he won't take my calls or return my texts.

The guys shake hands and greet us with a kiss on the cheek.

Except Mike.

He says hello with an awkward half-wave and immediately makes an excuse to walk away.

I feel so small.

All the blood drains from my face as everyone looks at me with sympathy, making me feel more insignificant. I look down at the floor again, feeling rejected.

God, please help me!

I recover as quickly as I can and smile coyly, trying to disguise my humiliation.

I didn't do anything wrong.

Jack and Mario give me a mercy grin but don't say anything. I'm grateful for their discretion, because we have never really built a rapport.

My embarrassment is clear, so I make a quick getaway to the bar.

"Are you okay?" Marie is by my side in seconds.

"No, he just walked away. He might as well

have slapped me," I say, feeling sorry for myself.

The bartender is busy, but I get his attention, "Vodka tonic, please." He rewards me with a kind wink, as if he knows how much I need that drink.

"I thought maybe he'd be here, but I wasn't sure. I told Sam this might not be a good idea, but he insisted. Bastard, I'm going to kill him!" Marie's piercing eyes are fixated like lasers on Sam, as he approaches.

"It was bound to happen. I had to see him someday," I attempt to calm her down.

She pulls Sam by the jacket and lets him have it. "I told you this was a bad idea. Why do I listen to you? Fix this!"

Sam glares apprehensively at her, then at me. He can't afford to piss her off, not if he's going to make any headway.

"I'm sorry. But listen, you have to get over it," he squeaks at me.

Not quite the answer I was expecting.

His hazel eyes are pleading with me not to make a bigger deal of this awkward situation.

I sense he knows something I don't.

Have they talked about me?

"What do you know? Has he said something to you?" I plead with him for any morsel of information.

He shakes his head, his hands in his pants' pockets, and he shrugs. "I don't know anything.

And it's not my place."

He does know something. Traitor!

"I thought you were my friend. If you know something, please tell me," I implore.

He looks torn but won't admit to anything. "I don't know. But as your friend, I'm advising you to let it go."

Let it go? Let it go! Has he met a girl before? Girls can't let anything go! We have to know!

I feel like I'm running out of time to finish a jigsaw puzzle, and he knows exactly where the pieces fit but won't tell me.

"Seriously, Sam, if you know something..." insists Marie.

"I really don't," he replies, taking her hand to try to calm her down.

The bartender hands me the drink. I take a sip, look up, and see Mike. He's back with Jack and Mario sharing a good laugh. He doesn't seem to have a care in the world.

So, it's just me that's falling apart.

After the way he's treated me, that shouldn't surprise me.

I decide to go talk to him, but as soon as I take a few steps, Sam grabs me by the arm.

"Don't," he pleads.

I frown at him. If he won't tell me what he knows, I will find out myself. I pull my arm from his grasp and keep walking. Marie follows quietly behind me.

"Damn," he sneers.

"Hi," I say hopeful, as I walk up to Mike and his friends.

"Hi!" Jack and Mario respond in unison.

Before I can utter another word, Mike interrupts. "I have to go," he says sharply and walks away.

What the hell!

He's just put me on display again. I've become the pathetic girl that's hung up on him. The tragic person he wants nothing to do with. He actually left the wedding and his friends, rather than be in the same room with me.

This is the guy I love. The guy I've been crying for...

"Why do you love him, sweetie? He's kind of an ass. What do you see in him? Please explain it to me." My best friend Rob Bellatorre's harsh words come to mind.

"I obviously don't know him that well, but I can see who he is."

Rob has only met Mike over FaceTime, but I've shared with him every detail of our relationship. I had often thought about that comment with some resentment toward Rob.

What had he seen that I didn't...or chose not to see?

Jackass!

I'm peeved and determined to find out who he is and what he's made of. I'm going to get my answers once and for all!

"I have to talk to him," I say to Marie.

"But he just left," scoffs Sam, pointing to the exit. "That should tell you everything you need to know!"

Jack and Mario politely excuse themselves.

I'm glad they left. This fairy-tale-gone-dark has nothing to do with them. The only reason Sam is involved is because he's chasing after Marie and hangs out with us all the time.

Mario seems to be the quiet one, but I've never said more than "hello" to him.

And Jack...well, I've just heard stories about Jack, but I've never said more than two words to him.

Marie gawks at Sam, essentially shutting him up. "What do you want to do?" she turns to me.

"Go to his apartment, knock on his door, and make him talk to me," I say firmly.

Sam rolls his eyes in disgust.

I don't care. As long as Marie has my back, I'm good.

"Let's go," she affirms.

CHAPTER 3

FOUR MONTHS AGO, CONT...

On the way to his apartment, Marie is quiet —
very much unlike her. Sam is driving and
turns his head to take a quick peek at me.

"What are you going to do?" he questions me
with trepidation.

"I have to talk to him. I need to know why."

We're parked outside of Mike's place. He's definitely home, because his car is here, and the lights
in his apartment are on.

He lives in a small studio on the first floor of a
six-apartment building. He's in his second year of
graduate school, working on his masters in political
science, and money is tight.

"Are you sure about this?" asks Sam, hoping I'll
change my mind.

"Yes," I reply with absolute determination.

Their eyes follow me, as I exit the car.

I have to do this, I have to do this, I CAN DO THIS!

I walk toward his front door with a steady resolve, an unwavering purpose, and knock.

It doesn't take long. He opens the door, and there he stands: tall, slim, dark hair, olive skin, brown eyes, and those lips...those full lips that have kissed me so many times.

"Our lips are made for each other," I whisper as we're kissing, "they fit perfectly together."

"Yes, they do," he replies.

Gut-wrenching memory!

"Hi," he says, stunned to see me standing at his door.

He doesn't invite me in. Another blow to my already shattered ego, but I stand my ground.

"We need to talk," I say, ice in my voice but dying inside.

"What is there to say?" he responds blasé and stares at the floor.

"Why? What happened, Mike? You just walked away, without a word. Don't I deserve more?"

I wish he'd look at me, but he does not.

He's leaning on the door frame, his arm

stretched out holding the door open, still looking down. The black pants and blue shirt are gone. He's now wearing jeans, a white T-shirt, and no shoes.

My heart is beating out of my chest, my pulse racing with the adrenaline coursing through my body. My stomach is in knots, and I fear my resolve is about to betray me, as I fearfully wait for his response.

He finally looks up and stares into the distance. There is emptiness in his eyes. It's hard to witness.

"We just grew apart. We don't see each other enough. You were across the country living and studying in Chicago, and I'm here. Plus, I've seen other people..." he trails off.

I examine him, taking in his words. I break them down syllable by syllable, trying to find clues to what I have done wrong, looking for the signs to when my misstep led him to walk away from us.

I feel overcome and struggle to figure out what I'm doing here, praying I don't fall apart in front of him.

I have just graduated from college, and moved to Los Angeles to be closer to him and to live with Marie. I met him three years ago, when I was visiting Marie on Christmas break, and it had been Mike and Ellie ever since.

This was supposed to be our chance to finally be together full time, to break the distance and time constraints, to move our relationship forward, to...

Clearly, those were my wishes not his.

"I've seen other people too," I respond, trying to abate the sting of his confession.

He finally looks at me, wide-eyed, dismayed.

"I understood that during the time we were apart, you'd do your thing and I would do mine. No questions, no explanations. But it was always you and me at the end of the day," I finish.

He's gaping at me like I've grown two heads.

That hurt him? Really?

His ego is hurt.

Well, my heart is broken!

"I just think the distance did us in," he recovers and looks at the floor again, like a coward, a quitter trying to pass his excuses off as facts. "You know, long distance relationships don't work, not really and..."

Why didn't he break up with me before? Why did he wait until we were living in the same city? Why didn't he break up with me in person? Why just walk away and ignore me? Why?

I study him one last time while he speaks, burning to my memory those dreamy eyes that will never gaze into mine again, the lips that will never kiss mine, the hair I will never run my hands through, the hands that will never hold me. And all I hear is static noise in the form of bullshit coming out of his mouth.

In this instant, I love him and hate him.

I'm not going to get the answers I'm looking for, and I've had enough. I feel sick, literally sick. I fear I will pass out.

I have to end this charade, now.

"I wasted so much time loving you...for this! Goodbye, Mike," I utter with contempt and quickly walk away.

I'm trying to keep a normal pace, but inside I'm running toward the car. Marie is gaping at me from the front seat of Sam's black Honda Accord. Her eyes wide, in awe that I'm still standing, and ready to jump out of the car to catch me if I fall.

I open the back door and get in.

"Let's go," I say quietly.

Marie turns back to look at me, dumbfounded.

"What happened?" asks Sam, trying to catch a glimpse of me through the rearview mirror as we drive away.

"We talked," I reply and let the tears flow.

I'm sobbing like a small child, feeling the weight of the world around me, the loss, my foolishness, and his indifference.

I can't handle so many disillusions at once.

He is my first grown-up love. The first guy I made love to. The only guy I have made love to because he is — *was* — the one. Three years of my life spent loving someone who didn't love me.

I feel shattered, played, and ridiculous!

"What did you expect? Did you need a neon

sign on his forehead telling you it's over?" blurts Sam.

Fuck, thanks a lot!

Guys and their lack of sympathy...

"Shut up, Sam, and take us home!" barks Marie.

CHAPTER 4

I stand under the warm water a bit longer. It's really over. It's been four months since I spoke with him, five since he left me. Confronting him changed nothing. His words were hogwash, and there's nothing I can do about it.

Now if I could just find a balm to temper the cold in my chest, that dark and bottomless pit that now lives where my heart used to be.

The cure is in my hands. Marie has reminded me enough times.

"You have to love yourself more, Ellie. You have to help yourself, Ellie. You can do better than him, Ellie. You deserve better, Ellie."

I need a way out of this labyrinth of melancholy I'm lost in.

Marie is still in my bedroom when I get out of the shower.

Has she been here the whole time?

"Just wanted to make sure you're okay. You know, make sure you hadn't drowned yourself in the shower," she mocks.

I roll my eyes.

"It's been way too long since you 'confronted' him, Ellie, four eternal months, and it's gotten you nowhere. These stints in bed have to stop!"

Her hands are on her hips, as she's scolding me. Lovingly but scolding me...again.

"I know, I promise I'm trying," I say to placate her. "I was just remembering the day I 'confronted' him," I imitate her air quotes. "I can't believe I actually stood there in front of him, defiant, demanding an explanation. But, God, inside I was falling apart, Marie, begging him to reconsider."

I shake my head in disbelief. I can still feel the anxiety I felt that day.

"I'm glad I didn't give him the satisfaction of seeing me fall apart. At least I have that," I sigh.

"I can't believe it either," she admits. "That was one brave ass move, Ellie."

But she's not done with me and begins her lecture.

"Where's that fearlessness now? It's time to prove to yourself, not him, the kind of woman you are. I know you're smart, strong, resilient, loving, beautiful, and so much more. But do you? Have you forgotten? If you don't get back to the land of the living, Ellie, you might as well have dropped to your knees in front of him and begged him to take you back."

Damn, she's harsh!

Relationships seem to come easy to her. She's a petite, beautiful, outgoing girl, with lovely olive skin and long, dark hair, a firecracker that you don't want to mess with. She's never been hurt this badly, and I don't wish it on her.

She's right. Where have I gone? I gave Mike the best of me, and he threw it away. The rational side of my brain is screaming at me to take back my shattered self and fix it.

Get off your ass and get back to living, Ellie!

The rational side of me has a point.

"Well, if you're done berating me," I give her a weak smile and a wink. "Can we go out for lunch now?"

She exhales sharply, "Good girl!"

CHAPTER 5

Marie has been on my case every weekend. She's been keeping me busy and distracted, so I don't stay in bed moping over Mike.

It's been a month since my last stint in bed.

Today, she's dragged me to NORMS for breakfast, and we hit the .99 Cent store for kitchen and bathroom essentials. We're home by late morning and have put everything away.

I still feel a bit numb at times, but I remind myself that life goes on. It will go on, whether I'm part of it or not.

Do I want to spend the next year completely unaware and oblivious to life, stuck on the loss of a love that was probably never mine in the first place? Or do I move on, as best as I can, one day at a time, making the best of every day?

I choose the latter, because as overwhelming as the loss of Mike feels, losing a year of my life, or even another day, sitting around wishing for someone who will not come back to me is foolish and just too high of a price to pay.

I haven't arrived at this conclusion solely on my own. Marie and Rob have been there for me every step of the way, patiently holding my hand through every bout of depression. I'm very lucky they love me so much and have been so patient.

All those plans I had when I thought I'd be sharing them with Mike are still viable. I just have to tweak them to work solely for myself, and slowly but surely, I'm becoming okay with that.

I'm even getting back to social media, after shunning it for half a year. I hadn't had the strength to see anything related to Mike. To watch him move on, happy, living his life without me was too much to handle. Why torture myself further?

Instagram is my social media distraction at the moment. I'm checking one of my favorite accounts, when Marie walks into my bedroom.

"Sam texted me and wants to go out," she shows me her iPhone. "I think you should come too. I mean, pity-weekends may be behind you, but you can certainly use a good distraction," she says, with a tinge of sarcasm.

"So go. He wants to see you, not me."

"Oh no, I'm not going to leave you here to somehow rationalize that it's okay to get back into bed and start another pity-party. Please come with us," she pleads with me.

"I'm not a child, Marie," I blurt out. "I'll keep myself busy."

"Stop acting like one and I'll stop worrying about you," she counters.

Ouch, Miss Know-it-all!

The last thing I want is to feel like a third wheel, and I tell her so.

"You're never a third wheel, and you certainly won't be one tonight."

"What does she mean?" I wonder aloud.

"Jack is coming with. In fact, he's driving."

Jack? I barely know him. I don't even remember what he looks like.

"Driving where and why Jack?" I ask confused.

Marie gives me a sly gaze and heads to my closet to rummage.

"Can I borrow this?" She holds up my new, black, cropped top.

"Of course." I don't know why she's asking. Half my clothes are already in her closet — my tops anyway, because the bottoms are too long for her.

"Answer me. Why Jack?"

She explains that Sam knows she'll only go out if I come along, and he suggested Jack could join us.

"So I won't feel like the third wheel," I interrupt her.

"Well, yea, but it's not like that. Besides, he's sweet. You're really going to like him."

All I know about Jack are the off-hand comments I've heard Mike make.

"Jack's got the ladies eating out of his hands." Or *"Women love Jack, doesn't hurt he's got a nice car."*

From what I've heard Mike and Sam say, they consider Jack the "stunner" of the four. I'm not sure why they've given him that moniker, since they're all good looking in their own way.

To me, Mike is the hot one, obviously.

As hard as I try to remember him, I have no idea what Jack looks like...strange.

My mood's been much better lately, but can I take a night out with someone I don't really know?

Hmm, small talk with "stunner" Jack?

It can't go any worse than the last time I went out with her and Sam, the disastrous wedding that led to the confrontation with Mike.

Marie is insisting that I come, when her cell pings with a text.

"Sam is asking if it's a go. They'll pick us up at 7:00 p.m. I won't go without you," she stresses.

She really wants to see Sam, and I don't want to spoil her plans. I hear my iPhone ping.

Sam: You better say yes Ellie!

Damn, now Sam's on my case!

Marie grins, because she knows he just texted me.

"Fine, I'll go, but I can't guarantee that I'll be good company. You may be asking for it," I say playfully.

"Ha, you put up with me, I put up with you. That's how it works, muñe."

I laugh and make faces at her, because as exasperating as she can be, her intentions are always good.

࿐࿐࿐

I've succeeded at hiding my dark circles and have made my best attempt to style my hair. I've always looked well put together, but the last six months have been a challenge in that department. If I wash my face and moisturize, I consider it a victory.

I've put much less effort into my wardrobe, jeans, a faded blue T-shirt, and old, black Vans sneakers. Marie is also in jeans, but she's wearing the cropped top she borrowed earlier.

"Where exactly are we going?" I ask.

Maybe I should rethink the Vans.

"To a bar in Santa Monica to watch the fight. The guys are deciding which one, don't worry about it. We'll have fun."

The fight?

"I don't even like boxing," I mumble to myself.

"It's not about the boxing but the company," she peers at me from under her lashes.

Yikes, I didn't mean for her to hear that.

The doorbell rings.

Here we go.

❧❧❧

Sam is leaning against a black Mercedes Benz AMG C63 S sedan that's parked in front of our house, his arms folded. He's gone all out to impress Marie, dark jeans, plum shirt, dressy sneakers, hair nicely styled, and he smells fantastic.

"Hello, beautiful ladies," he gives each of us a kiss on the cheek, though Marie gets an extra hug.

Jack is standing by the driver's door.

This must be his car.

Marie walks over to him and greets him with a kiss on the cheek. He tosses a grin in my direction and gives me a half-wave. I reply in kind. He quickly gets in the car and turns on the engine.

"You go in the front with Jack," Sam instructs.

"No, please, I don't know him," I whimper mortified.

He looks from me to Marie, back at me, and

finally takes pity. He asks if I'd like him to ride with me in the back. I nod yes.

Marie beams at him sweetly. "Thank you, Sam," she says softly.

He smiles at her, then opens the back door for me and the front for her.

CHAPTER 6

It's a short ride from Culver City to Santa Monica, so we'll get to the bar in no time.

Jack doesn't make an attempt to speak to me, nor I to him. He's in deep conversation with Marie about their mutual jobs.

Marie is bragging about her job as a graphic designer at a boutique ad agency. She has every right to boast, it's a pretty sweet gig. Jack, apparently, manages a chain of upscale coffee shops.

"Jack is wicked smart, great with numbers. I don't know why he didn't get an MBA," I recall Mike saying once.

Sam is extra sweet to me. I feel at ease with him, as he keeps me company in the back seat.

"You have such nice hair," I say to him, trying

to be sociable and extend my hand to touch it. It's light brown, almost ash-blond, and very soft.

"I know," he answers and playfully rests his head on my lap.

"Do make yourself at home," I tease, running my hand through his hair.

"I'm glad you came out with us," he responds, looking up at me smiling, and I sense he means it.

಄಄಄

"We're here," Jack announces, as he parks the car.

Marie walks alongside Jack toward Sonny McLean's, while Sam and I follow behind them.

An Irish pub to watch a fight? Go figure.

It's early, and we get a table right away.

"This place gets pretty noisy sometimes," says Jack, "but it'll do to watch the fight."

I nod and take a seat next to Marie.

"Drinks, beer?" asks Jack.

I don't know much about beer and rarely, if ever, drink the stuff. Sam notices my hesitation and immediately offers his expertise, "Stella is a good choice."

We all approve, and Jack takes care of ordering. The beers arrive with enough food to feed ten people.

I'm trying hard to be present, to enjoy the moment, and join in the conversation, but I'm finding it difficult to escape my reveries of Mike. It doesn't take much to pull me into the abyss of my subconscious, a rerun of my memories eternally on auto replay. I catch myself and get back to sipping my beer and eating fries.

Between reaching for fries and taking small sips of beer, I catch Jack watching me. He gives me a polite smile, and I respond with a small grin.

He must think I'm an asshole, a tragic, sad little person he's been forced to tolerate.

I don't care.

He seems nice, though. I haven't heard him make any comments about Mike or the horrible wedding fiasco. I wonder if girls really do take to him. Mike made it sound like he was a stud with a nice car. He doesn't seem arrogant enough to be a player, but then, I've only given him a couple of glances.

"Are you okay?" whispers Marie.

"Sure, I'm enjoying my beer, and these fries are fantastic!" I respond with an extra huge smile, making her laugh.

"Well, at least you're eating. Any interest in joining the conversation?"

I shake my head no and get back to my food.

Most of the night is a haze.

I don't know who won the fight. I don't even know who was fighting. I'm just buzzed from two beers, and riding home in the back seat with Sam, softly singing Alejandro Sanz's "Siempre Es de Noche," which is playing in the car.

かかか

"Good night," says Jack. He gives Marie a kiss on the cheek, and I get another awkward wave.

I don't blame him.

I grab the keys from my purse, walk in the house, and head for my bedroom. Marie walks in a few minutes later.

"That was nice, wasn't it?" She sits on the corner of my bed, her expression hopeful that I had a good time, despite my zombie-like state the entire night.

I wish I could say it was a fun night for me too, but the truth is I remember very little of it.

"It was good," I lie.

I'm on my bed with my legs crossed, pretending to be exploring an app on my iPhone. I don't want to look at her. Maybe she'll believe me and let me be.

She doesn't.

"Come on, Ellie, you have to *want* to be okay. You're telling me even Jack's beautiful eyes didn't get you out of your Mike-coma for one second?"

What beautiful eyes?

I look up at her frowning, because I truly have no idea what she's talking about.

"OMG, Ellie! You didn't notice his eyes?" she's

practically shouting at me.

"No," I reply sulking and perplexed.

"You were sitting across from him all night. You mean to tell me you didn't look at him once?" she's exasperated, throwing her hands up in the air.

"Sorry. I didn't notice his eyes. I didn't notice the decorations on the walls. I didn't notice the waitress. I didn't notice if we sat at a table or a booth. I didn't notice the time we left. I didn't notice anything. I was there, but I wasn't. I'm sorry," I cover my face with my hands, so she won't see me tear up like a sullen child.

"Ellie, I...I'm sorry. I just wanted you to get out, join civilization again and maybe forget about Mike for one second," she tries to console me.

"No, I'm sorry. You're right," I reassure her, take a deep breath and wipe the few tears that escaped my eyes.

I may not care that Jack, Sam or the world thinks I'm a mess, but I have to try harder. I'm doing the best I can. But I'm like an addict, stuck in a toxic merry-go-round, where the memories of Mike are holding me prisoner.

No. *I'm* holding myself prisoner. I've chained myself to the flashbacks of Mike kissing me, holding me, touching me. I've trapped myself in a warped world of self-pity and grief.

Marie is just trying to help me see the light. She's always been there for me. She invited me to live with her, when I told her I wanted to move to LA. Her parents own this house, so I don't have to worry about the high cost of living in the area. Everything was going as planned, until Mike decided otherwise. For my own sake, I have to let him go!

"Why are you asking me about Jack's eyes anyway?" I say with a coy smile, trying to lighten the mood.

"Muñeca, please, you have to look next time. I guarantee it's worth it," she winks at me.

Next time? Who said there'll be a next time?

"He's one of Mike's best friends," I respond, wondering why Jack's eyes are even a topic of conversation.

"I know. I'm not suggesting anything. I'm just saying he has nice eyes," she stands to leave. "Sleep well, Ellie," she blows me a kiss and walks out.

"You too, Marie, I love you," I shout back.

CHAPTER 7

I've thought a lot about that night at the Irish pub. I felt so lost, even in the presence of friends. It's a shame that I can't enjoy a night out, or genuinely smile, and have a conversation with friends. It's sad that I put myself in that position and continue to succumb to self-inflicted pain.

Poor Jack. *He* was the third wheel that day, because I wasn't really there. I made the worst impression anyone can make, and yet, I never felt any judgment or even contempt from him.

I wonder what's behind those beautiful eyes...

Though admittedly, I only think they're beautiful because Marie says so. I have to remember to look at them, if I ever see him again.

I've promised myself to be present from now on

with Jack or with anyone I meet. Mike is still on my mind, though not as intensely as before, and that's an improvement. I've come to terms with the fact that he didn't love me.

Damn, it hurts to admit it, but it's the truth.

The day will come when his name means nothing to me. I swear it will.

As I let him go, I'm regaining my self-confidence and becoming the determined Ellie I once was. I'm starting to take my life back, and it's about damn time.

I can't do anything about the pathetic state of my love life, but I can work on my career. I'm determined to succeed on that front. I'm occupying my days and nights bringing my career plans to fruition. That's a better use of my time than letting my hours be consumed by thoughts of my broken heart.

My part time job at RedBrick Records, an established indie label located in Santa Monica, has been a godsend. Rob hooked me up soon after I arrived in LA. He knows Dan Thomas, the VP of Marketing, and got wind there was a coordinator position available. His friendship with Dan got me in the door for an interview, but I earned the job.

The best part is that the label's offices are only a few blocks from Marie's job. She drops me off in the morning, since I don't have my own car yet, and I take public transportation back.

As a marketing coordinator, I'm assisting Dan and learning the business. He's very young, maybe 10 years older than me, sharp, knowledgeable, and demanding but fair.

I love the fast pace, the deadlines, and the high energy of this job. The office is full of young people, who like me, are fighting to make their way in this cutthroat and competitive business of entertainment.

I've even made new friends. It's great to have people to banter with, to share water cooler stories about artists, and just have a good laugh.

This job, together with a freelance gig for a local music magazine back home in Chicago, are keeping me somewhat solvent at the moment. But I have to find a full-time job soon, because the bills are adding up, and my current salary won't cut it for long.

Dan is constantly praising my dedication and hard work. He's mentioned he'd like to promote me to a full time position when one becomes available. But he's also made it quite clear that it's unlikely to happen any time soon, because record labels are somewhat struggling at the moment. I'm hopeful the opportunity opens up, but I can't sit around waiting.

With that in mind, I've been spending all my off time searching full-time opportunities online. I've sent at least twenty resumes to entertainment and music magazines, radio stations, concert promoters, and other music related agencies.

And maybe, just maybe, my hard work has paid off.

Of all the resumes I've sent thus far, I'm most excited about an editor opportunity at an entertainment magazine. This is where my college internships and freelance work have come in handy, because I've landed an interview.

The location on the original job post said LA/NY. I don't know what that means exactly, but I'm looking forward to finding out, when I meet with them.

❧❧❧

My days have morphed into a tedious routine of waking up, coffee, work, lunch, home, sending resumes, dinner, catch up with Marie, sleep.

Though catch up time with Marie is less of a catch up and more of a, *"How are you today, Ellie? Are you feeling better today, Ellie? Have you managed not to cry today, Ellie?"* kind of deal.

I've tried to assure her that crying is no longer on the menu, but I can't hide the nostalgia that assaults me from time to time. I am making progress though, reminding myself *I* have the answers to my distress.

I'm walking out of my office, saying goodbye to Lola, the receptionist, when I hear my iPhone ping.

It's probably Marie.

This morning she mentioned she might leave work early and suggested another catch up. I hope this time it includes wine, because it's Friday, and I'm done putting up with her interrogations about my mood, if I'm sober.

> **Marie: Muñe what's up for tonight?**
> **Ellie: Thought you wanted to do girls' night**
> **Marie: For sure! Heading home early. Drinks, dinner, boys (friends)?**
> **Ellie: Drinks and dinner yes! Boys no**
> **Marie: 😄😄... I'll bring the food you get the wine**
> **Ellie: Done! 😄**

಄಄಄

I'm softly singing along to Gwen Stefani's kick ass tune, "Used to Love You," that's playing on my iPhone, while setting up the coffee table in the living room for our catch up dinner.

"How apt," observes Marie.

She's looking at me with a cautious smile, hoping I'm not going to cry my way through the roasted chicken. I smile back embarrassed at my unintentional musings and tendency to sing, when I think no one is listening. That song just gets to me. Lately, every song gets to me.

"I'm not going to begin sobbing, if that's what

you mean. Don't worry," I roll my eyes, laugh, and sit on the floor.

I am doing better, I am trying harder, and I am succeeding at tolerating the memories of my old life. I can't say the sun is fully shining for me just yet, because that's going to take time, but things are looking up.

"Just making sure or I will be forced to replace your music list with mine, and you know me, it's bump-and-grind all the way," she teases and begins twerking right in front of my face.

I let out a huge laugh, the first loud, stomping-feet laugh I've had in months. I'm clutching my aching stomach, unable to stop laughing, and trying to push her behind away from me.

Her grinding and lewd faces only make me laugh harder, so much so I begin snorting, as tears start rolling down my face.

She stops immediately.

"No, no, don't cry," she begs softly.

"They're happy tears, silly," I slap her invading hands away. "You look like a cartoon when you twerk. How do you even get so low?" I gabble between laughing sobs.

"Low center of gravity, baby," she laughs with me, assured I am actually enjoying myself.

Her huge, radiant smile reminds me of all the love in my life. She loves me, she's my best friend. Rob loves me too. My parents and sisters love me.

I am a likeable, loveable person. I'm sure eventually another guy will love me, and I will love him. I have to remember that, and stay in that frame of mind, as I move forward with my life.

We're sitting on the floor, our legs crossed under the coffee table, and I refill our wine glasses. We are already on our second bottle and picking at leftovers.

"Watch out, I'm about to pop these babies open," Marie unbuttons her jeans and lets out a big burp.

"Oops, sorry," she peels her eyes at me, laughing at her unladylike behavior.

We've eaten way too much, and my stomach has expanded at least three inches.

Sheesh, I'm glad I'm wearing leggings.

CHAPTER 8

"So, tell me how you're doing," Marie begins the after dinner interrogation.

Oh no, not more of this.

I have to make it clear to her that I am better.

Not only am I done with the, "*How are you today, Ellie?*" cross-examinations, but I also need her to stop worrying so much. My problems aren't hers, and she shouldn't have to take them on or walk on eggshells around me.

"Can I say something, just to put your mind at ease?"

"Shoot," she replies.

"Let me start by saying I appreciate you so much. You've taken care of me so well, Marie. You've protected me, even from myself, and I'm forever grateful. I know I've made it hard for you, and that you've somehow taken on my problems as your own. Please don't do that anymore. I assure you that I'm better."

"But I worry," she interrupts me. "I see how sad you still are sometimes, and the light in your eyes is gone."

"I know, but that's just going to take time. You have to concede that I'm doing so much better than I was even a month ago. I'm really trying for my sake, and even for yours. It may look like I'm taking baby steps, but they're important steps, because what I went through with Mike devastated me. I'm putting the pieces of my life back together, and I'm using glue, fucking Krazy Glue. I swear! I promise I'll be more than okay once I'm all back together. I know you'll be there for me if I stumble, and you have no idea how much knowing that helps in my recovery. I know you'll drag me out of bed by my hair, if I dare go back to pitying myself," I giggle, eyeing her.

She moves her head from side to side, twisting her mouth in the same direction, brooding over my last comment, and asserting that's exactly what she'll do if I regress. Her comical face makes me giggle more.

"I may stumble again," I continue, "but I promise I'll immediately get up, dust myself off, and keep going. I'm meeting new people, making new friends, and going out. That's a huge improvement from where I was. Now I just want us to get back to our usual fun-loving selves, because that will help me a lot more than discussing how I'm feeling every time we have dinner. I swear you'll be the first to know when I'm feeling like crap. You will also be the first to know when I'm feeling better. And I am, so there. Now you know," I look at her with hopeful eyes, praying she understands I'm okay.

I want to be as good of a friend to her as she's been to me. I must make a conscious effort to watch my demeanor around her and not worry her with nonsense feelings that only I can change.

"See, that's the Ellie Valencia I know and love," she grins, happy to see me much more sure of myself.

"I do see that you're doing better, Ellie, and I'm glad," she begins. "Don't worry about me, please. I'm not taking on your problems, not at all. I'm your friend, your sister, and that's what family does. It's my job to be there for you, because you have been there for me too. Remember in 2nd grade when I was devastated because my crush, Charlie Ferrer, pulled my hair and yelled at me during recess, in front of the entire class, to stop looking at him? You pushed him so hard he fell to the ground. Then you fisted your hand at him and said, 'You think you're a man, don't you? You're a little boy, and if you yell at her or pull her hair again, I'll stomp on you!'"

We both blurt out a laugh remembering my first fight to defend Marie. Little Charlie left her alone, and she stopped looking at him.

"That's what you do. You're there for me too. How many of my sob stories have you heard? Going through high school in LA without you was tough. How many times did you talk me off the ledge, when some guy broke my teen heart? How many hours did you stay on the phone with me? Tons!" she gives me a funny pout.

"You wanted to jump on a plane when mom had that car accident, even after we knew she was okay and just had a broken arm. I wouldn't let you, so you stayed on the phone with me for hours, because I couldn't sleep from the anxiety. When I needed help with my college applications, you walked me through the process step by step. Any time I need advice, help, or comfort you drop everything to be there for me. I'm returning the favor, Ellie. You're very independent, and you like to do things on your own. I get that. But you can lean on me too. You're not going to break me, you're not imposing, and I can handle everything that comes our way. I can't push Mike to the ground and stomp him," she grins and fists her hand. "So taking care of you is the next best thing."

She's right, that's what friends do.

Mike leaving me increased my anxiety and fear of depending too much on other people. I have to realize that sometimes I do need help, sometimes I do need a shoulder to cry on, sometimes I can let people in, certainly Marie.

"Now that we got that straight," she says, "more wine?"

"Oh, hell yes!" I exclaim excitedly, happy to spend time with her now that we've both said our piece, and her interrogations are finally over.

"We have another bottle, and it's not going to go to waste," I smile at her. "I promise the light in my eyes is just behind a thin veil that will be completely gone soon. I'm working on it. Cross my heart. Now, show me how to twerk!"

She pops to her feet laughing and drags me with her.

CHAPTER 9

"Hey, princess, wake up!" Marie shouts, as she walks into my bedroom scratching her butt.

I open one eye to look at her and immediately burst into laughter.

She looks like a disheveled clown.

Her makeup is smudged all over her face, and her hair is a tornado of thick, dark locks scattered across the top of her head.

Ahh! I grab my throbbing head.

Ay, ay, ay those three bottles of wine last night might not have been our brightest idea.

"Whatcha laughing at, princess? You look no better than me," she laughs with me.

"Why are you up?" I giggle, still holding my aching head.

"Well, besides the fact that it's one in the after-noon," she mocks.

"Shut up!"

"Yep," she gives me an exaggerated nod, before walking out of my room.

"Sam texted. He wants to hit Busby's tonight," she shouts over her shoulder.

"Okay!"

She peeks into my room, "You said yes? Yay!" She smiles and taps the door in excitement.

"No, I said okay. What do I have to do with you going out with Sam? You said nothing about me coming along," I scoot out of bed.

I'm looking in the mirror, trying to wrangle in my long hair with a hair tie, and wiping my face with a wet towelette to remove yesterday's makeup.

"The invite is for both of us," she explains.

I doubt that very much, but I don't want to argue. I've been in really good spirits, as life and work are looking up, and hope is blooming.

"Mhm, show me the text," I challenge, teasing her.

Her eyes pop open, and she knows she's been caught.

I laugh at her.

"Weirdo! I know what you're up to, but I'm game. What time is he coming by?"

She giggles and returns to her room. "Eight," she shouts. "Jack's coming too. He'll meet us there."

Third wheel averted. Thank you, Jack!

❧❧❧

Busby's is already pretty crowded. Sam leads the way with Marie. They're holding hands and are very much into each other. I follow them to a bar table with high chairs.

"Jack should be here soon," Sam says. "He's coming straight from work, so he may not look his best. Please forgive him." He directs that last comment at me.

I shrug.

Why should I care what Jack looks like?

I ignore his remark.

"Beer, wine?" he asks.

Marie opts for a beer.

"Water with lemon for me," I respond.

He heads to the bar to get our drinks.

Marie pulls me in and whispers, "Sam looks really good tonight, doesn't he?"

I smile and nod yes.

"Hi, how's it going?" says a voice from behind.

It's Jack. He's wearing a gray shirt with tiny blue stripes, black pants, and a black leather jacket.

I don't know what Sam was talking about. He looks great to me.

"Hi," I grin back at him.

It's the first genuine smile I've given him. He's

surprised by my amicable welcome and gives me a candid grin.

"Where's Sam?" he asks, still regarding me.

I fold under his intense gaze and quickly look to Marie for assistance. She points to the bar, and Jack excuses himself to go find him.

As he walks away, I take him in for the first time. He's tall — at least 6'2" — slim, broad-shouldered, with fair skin lightly kissed by the sun, and short, wavy, raven hair — *hmm, that hair, very Orlando Bloom on the cover of InStyle.*

And his firm behind in those pants...

Whoa, stop staring at it, Ellie!

He walks with long, firm strides, like a man who knows where he's going, what he wants, and isn't afraid to go for it. There's a confident air about him, but it's not arrogance, despite the fact that women are gawking at him.

Myself included...

He and Sam talk while they wait for the drinks. Jack is leaning against the bar sideways facing Sam, who's laughing at something Jack's saying.

His side profile is striking — perfectly symmetrical features, straight nose and chiseled jaw, like a flawlessly sculpted work of art.

Better than any model I've seen in GQ.

I have to admit, the sight of him is...stunning.

He turns our way and catches me staring.

Damn!

He grins amiably, and quickly turns back to whatever entertaining exchange he's enjoying with Sam.

They're smiling when they get back to our table. It's apparent they share everything with each other — the good, the bad and the funny.

Jack hands me my drink. "Vodka tonic?" he asks, examining it.

"Water," I reply shyly.

He nods and mouths an almost silent, "Okay."

I don't know if he's making fun of me, but I let it slide. I'm determined that nothing, or anyone, will dampen my newfound good mood.

Sam is going on about the cheesy nicknames they had for each other when they were kids but won't share what they are.

"What's the point, if you don't tell us so we can laugh with you," I banter.

Jack turns to me with a coquettish smile. It's the first time he's heard me join in the conversation. He's amused.

I don't look at him long.

Yes, the ex-sourpuss girl does have a sense of humor.

"Because we don't want you laughing at our expense," replies Jack with a broad, playful grin.

I return the smile and briefly gaze at him, while I sip my water.

He quickly turns to Sam, "Right?" he prods.

"Back me up, Sam."

Sam's not interested in Jack's charms on display and is practically ignoring him. He's too busy having a staring contest with Marie.

"We'll never tell," Sam finally replies and gently kisses Marie on the cheek.

I know where that's heading and so does Jack, because he asks me to go with him to grab another drink. I agree and eagerly follow him.

The way to the bar is crowded, and not wanting to lose him in the throngs of people, I hold on to the back of his jacket. He feels the pull, gently grabs my arm and takes my hand. He weaves his long, strong fingers around mine.

When we get closer to the bar, he positions me in front of him, protecting me from crowd.

We wait patiently for our turn, and as the minutes creep by, he's getting closer and closer to me, moving me slightly forward toward the bar. I can feel his body all over mine, and his cologne fills my senses.

I don't know what it is, but it's...alluring.

Yes, very alluring!

I close my eyes briefly. I'm slightly captivated. He's so close to me, and I'm trying hard not to think about it.

"What do you want?" his warm breath tickles my ear.

I feel a delicious shiver in the back of my neck

that travels through my entire body. I swear I'm turning all shades of red.

"Eh..." I can't concentrate.

The bartender stares impatiently, while I sputter like a love struck teenager.

"Nothing thanks, maybe later."

Get a hold of yourself, Ellie. He's just being polite.

"Dos XX Lager with a lot of lime, please," he says to the bartender.

When he stretches past me to pay, he leans even closer. I instinctively hold on to the edge of the bar.

"You okay?" he asks gazing at me, one of his hands is now on the bar and the other on the small of my back.

"Mhm," I reply meekly.

I don't quite understand why his slightest touch is unsettling me, though not in a bad way. Deep down, this is very exciting. I'm struggling between putting a stop to it and just letting it be.

I decide on letting it be.

It's not like we're on a date. He's just being nice to me. I can use a little nice in my life.

He shifts to his side and leans on the bar, helping me do the same with a swift move of his hand on my back. We're now facing each other, and I'm smiling timidly at him, not really knowing why.

"So, you're not drinking tonight," he says with mirth.

I shrug, feeling shy.

He takes the lime and squeezes it into the Dos XX bottle, and then stretches past me to grab the salt, his face almost touches mine. I hold my breath, but he doesn't seem fazed and smiles.

Salt in hand, he proceeds to add some to his beer.

"It's called a michelada," he explains, giving me a playful stare, "beer, lots of lime and salt, though I have to settle for the few limes they gave me."

He's studying me.

I can't help but stare at his captivating smile.

My eyes follow the beer bottle as it reaches his mouth...he takes a drink.

That looks...yummy!

CHAPTER 10

"**W**ant a taste?" he offers, bringing me back to the here and now.

Is he flirting with me?

It takes me a second to realize he's just being gracious. I can use gracious.

I take the beer from his hand without saying a word and take a sip.

Mmm, it is good.

I hand the bottle back to him, and he takes another drink.

"What's your degree in, Ellie?"

"Music business management," I say with pride.

"Interesting. I hear you're working at a record label."

He hears...How?

"What genre of music are you hoping to ultimately work in?" he inquires and hands me the beer.

I take another sip and hand it back to him.

"How do you know I work at a record label?"

"Sam," he says. "I figured I should know something about you. I didn't want to seem rude and have nothing to talk about, should you choose to speak to me this time." He grins teasingly and takes a drink.

I behaved like a moronic zombie the first time we went out. Of course he thinks I'm rude. This is my chance to change his impression of me, and show him I'm actually a very nice, attentive, and fun person.

"I'm sorry. I didn't mean to be rude to you last time," I look at him briefly, before my confidence falters.

"I wouldn't say rude, just...quiet." He hands me the beer.

His response makes me feel a little better about our first outing at that pub.

He doesn't think I'm rude. How does he do that, instantly make me feel better about myself?

"So, your degree, it's not a traditional choice. Are you hoping to make music at some point?" he questions.

I take a drink and hand the bottle back to him. He's examining me closely. I'm looking everywhere but directly at him, because he's making me nervous.

"No, not really. I'm not exactly musically gifted. I'm just interested in the music business and want to be involved behind the scenes," I halfway roll my eyes, desperately trying to escape his gaze. It's too intense, like he can see through all my walls. I stare at the beer instead.

"I see," he says, still watching me.

This time he doesn't immediately hand me the beer. He notices I'm eyeing it and playfully passes it to me. Then he motions the bartender. "Dos XX, lots of lime on the side."

Maybe he's done sharing his beer with me. The thought is displeasing.

"I think you're musical. I've heard you sing along to the radio," he smirks.

I think he might be taunting me.

Ugh, I do tend to do that. How embarrassing!

The bartender places another beer and more limes on the bar, but Jack ignores them. Instead, he focuses on the beer I'm holding. He takes it and swiftly drinks the last of it. He places the empty bottle on the bar, prepares the new one, and hands it to me.

I smile relieved, take a drink, and my eyes involuntarily land on his lips.

They look so tasty...

Stop staring at them, Ellie!

"That doesn't mean I have musical talent. It

just means I can follow along to a song that's well sung by someone with real talent," I say amused at myself.

He doesn't respond and instead just takes the beer.

I move my gaze to the collar of his shirt. It's a safer bet than his fleshy, kissable lips.

"How about you?" It's his turn to disclose some details about himself, *Mr. Women-love-him Jack.*

I look at him fleetingly.

He's grinning.

"Oh, I can't sing to save my life," he teases, making me giggle.

Hmm, and he's funny...

"I meant, what do you do? I hear you're great with numbers."

"Is that so?" he frowns, holding the beer mid-air to his mouth. "Says who?"

"Unimportant," I reply quickly.

Damn him and his lips!

"Oh," he's taken aback, maybe realizing it was Mike. "Well, I am," he grins proudly, "or at least I like to think so. I've done pretty well."

He takes a long sip and hands the bottle back to me.

"You manage businesses?" I inquire and quickly add, "Marie, tells me."

"Yes, several coffee shops, and we're expanding," he eyes the idle beer in my hand, and I quickly hand it back to him.

"Interesting," I mirror his previous comment to me, teasing him.

His mouth twists in amusement, and he takes a drink.

"Why did you decide to move to LA?" he hands me the beer.

I don't want to lie to him, but I also don't want to tell him Mike was part of the reason. I'm sure he already knows that, plus I don't want to sour our pleasant conversation.

I opt for a half-truth.

"This is the mecca of the record business. Well, here and New York. And although my best friend, Rob, lives in New York, Marie is like my sister. I thought the transition would be easier with her. Plus, you can't beat the weather."

I'm over clarifying, because his damn lips are making me so nervous, and I'm trying to avoid saying the name *Mike* at all costs. I don't think he notices, and if he does, he's kindly giving me a pass.

"That makes sense," he grins and takes the beer from my hand, allowing his fingers to brush softly against mine. He's getting feisty and flirtatious.

"Have you ever lived anywhere else?" I ask, absentmindedly twisting a strand of hair with my fingers, the nervous energy getting the best of me.

"No, but I wouldn't mind moving, provided I

had a good reason to," he replies self-assured, as he takes my fingers away from my hair. He holds them gently for the briefest of moments and then hands me the bottle.

I gaze at his lips, as my mind wanders, *"Wow, he just did that..."*

"And your family, are they all back in Chicago?" he asks.

I take a drink of the beer and come back to earth.

"Yes. Yours?" I quickly hand him back the bottle and take a deep breath. I let it out slowly. I don't know if it's the alcohol that's getting to me, or my impulse to kiss his beautiful lips.

"All in California."

He takes a drink and hands me the bottle. I take a tiny sip and immediately give it back.

"Do you have any siblings?" he inquires.

"Two sisters, much older than me. You?"

"A younger sister. Are your sisters as beautiful as you?" he takes a drink, eyeing me with a coy, flirty grin.

He thinks I'm beautiful? Maybe he is flirting with me. Why is that pleasing?

I shrug embarrassed by his compliment and smile back. If I say yes, I'll sound vain. If I say no, I'll still sound conceited, because he's going to think I'm saying I'm the only pretty one. All three of us are beautiful in our own way, but that's too long of an explanation. Besides, the opportunity for a sensible answer has passed, because the look he's giving me is making me blush tomato red.

We go on and on like this for the next hour, both of us sharing one bottle of beer.

He's attentive, engaging, and charming.

Why didn't I know this? Why hadn't I ever spoken to him before?

But I already know the answer. I've been wearing blinders that had only one line of sight directly to Mike.

Now Jack has my full, undivided attention. I can't ignore the fact that he's Mike's best friend and what that could mean. I feel guilty I'm enjoying him so much, that he's making me feel so comfortable, that for the first time in a long while my past isn't front and center in my thoughts.

What is this? How is this happening?

"The bar sure looks like a good spot to be," jokes Marie.

She and Sam have made their way to us.

"Easy to get refills," I jest.

CHAPTER 11

It's past 11:00 p.m., and the music inside Busby's is loud and not appropriate for conversation. Marie's dancing and failing miserably at getting Sam to move along with her.

Jack just prepared another beer, but unlike before he doesn't hand it to me first. He takes a long drink...his eyes taunting me.

"Hey!" I playfully snatch the bottle from him mid-drink. The liquid drips from his mouth onto his shirt. He leans forward to wipe it. When he looks up at me, his eyes are lit up with playfulness and mischief. I'm laughing at him, holding the beer in my hand.

Before I know it, he reaches for me. He wraps his arm around my waist and pulls me tightly against him. I don't have a chance to react, when suddenly his lips are on mine.

He's kissing me.

His tongue is prodding me to respond. Strong, full, divine lips have taken me by surprise, and it's exhilarating. I let myself go and respond, enjoying the delicious taste of his mouth. I hold on to him with my free hand, which has made its way to the back of his neck and into his hair.

His supple lips are urgent and demanding.

My brain is on pause, while my lips are following his lead, and I'm lost in the moment.

But just as suddenly, he releases me.

No!

He quickly grabs the beer from my hand and takes a drink.

Holy crap! That was...unexpected and sexy as hell!

He's eyeing me with a salacious grin, having just bested me.

I'm smiling back at him like a dope, trying to recover from the taste of his lips.

More, please!

He's very much aware of what he just did. He knows my history with Mike but doesn't seem to care.

I can't stop staring at him, and then I notice them...Big, beautiful, mesmerizing bluish-gray eyes beneath long lashes examining me, and I sigh deeply because I finally understand what Marie meant.

I'm captivated.

I catch myself and quickly look at Marie and Sam.

Did they see what just happened?

Sam is facing away from us, and Marie is dancing with her eyes closed. They saw nothing, and a sense of relief washes over me.

Jack kissed me!

I'm giddy and can't help the thrill coursing through me.

He continues to share his beer with me, but neither of us says a word about the stolen kiss.

I want him to kiss me again, but I'm also scared he will, because there's too much at stake — he's my ex's friend.

Why did he kiss me in the first place? Does he actually like me?

I have to consult with Marie.

Sam asks Jack to order a few more drinks, and I see an opening to drag Marie to the ladies' room.

"What's up? You look like you just scored the last cookie in the cookie jar," she mocks, because I can't stop smiling like a loon.

I take a deep breath.

"Jack kissed me," I gush excitedly.

"What?" Her mouth pops open, "No!"

"Yep," I nod with the stupid grin still plastered

on my face.

"When?"

"Just now, when you were dancing with Sam," I confirm.

"I didn't see a thing!"

"Sam didn't either. He was facing away from us."

Thank God!

"Game plan," she's really into this. "I'll keep Sam distracted, don't worry."

I hesitantly burst her bubble, "Eh, I don't think it's going to happen again."

"Whatever, Jack's a really nice guy, Ellie. I'll keep Sam distracted just in case. Do whatever you want," she remains unfazed by my reluctance.

She's happy for me, but she knows all too well if Sam finds out, he's going to freak because his loyalty is not only to Jack but Mike as well.

ﮱﮱﮱ

By 1:00 a.m., we're heading home.

Jack in fact did not kiss me again, but he held my hand, when Sam wasn't looking, and was playful and attentive all night.

I'm hoping he doesn't think I didn't like the kiss, because I did.

I really did!

The valet pulls up with our cars, and I hastily say,

"I'll ride with Jack."

He gives me a perceptive smile and a wink and opens the car door for me. I don't know why, but I'm glad he's pleased that I'm riding home with him.

Sam is completely unaware of what's happening between us and couldn't care less. As far as he's concerned, he'll be alone in his car with Marie, and that's all he cares about.

Jack and I are driving home in silence. I'm too tired — *and delighted* — to risk saying anything that will ruin the night. He turns on the radio very low. Bruno Mars' "When I Was Your Man" is playing, and his sultry voice is going on about the love he lost to another man.

I'm facing my window, my head is resting on the headrest, and my eyes are closed. I'm contemplating everything that happened tonight.

Suddenly, I feel Jack's hand softly caressing my cheek. He's looking at me. I can feel his caring eyes like a soft, warm blanket. After a few seconds, he reaches down, grabs my hand, and holds it tenderly. I don't make a sound or move an inch.

I'm in awe of him, of his uninhibited warmth, but I'm bewildered. I don't know why he's doing this, why he's so affectionate to a girl that only today acknowledged his presence. His guileless touch means everything. I haven't felt genuine affection in a long time, and I crave it. I need it.

Maybe he's just being nice because he thinks I'm still unglued. Even so, everything he's done tonight feels sincere.

He's so disarming.

With a simple touch, he's given me hope that I can survive what's left of my sick addiction to Mike. I don't want him to let go of my hand, because right now, he's the medicine I desperately need for my vulnerable heart and bruised self-esteem.

He's holding me outside my front door, neither of us wants to let go. His arms around me feel safe, like an anchor I can hold on to in a storm. He pulls away only when he hears Sam's car approaching. He gently kisses me on the cheek and squeezes my hand.

I stand there for a moment, gazing into his earnest bluish-gray eyes, wondering what tonight means.

I give him a quick kiss on the side of his lips and say good night.

ॐ ॐ ॐ

"So, what else happened?" asks Marie.

We're sitting at the kitchen table, and I tell her about Jack's affection in the car. She's drinking a glass of water listening closely.

"Marie, why didn't I meet Jack before?" I ask,

genuinely intrigued.

"I think you did, you must have. He's always been there. You don't remember meeting him?"

I shake my head no.

"I'm not surprised. From the moment you met Mike, he was it for you."

"I suppose so," I say distracted. I'm in my head, trying to make sense of how I feel about what happened with Jack.

"I'm so confused and elated at the same time about tonight. What does it mean?" I share my bewilderment with her.

"What do you want it to mean?"

What? Why is she answering me with a question?

"I need your advice, Marie. I've gone over every single detail of this night in my head, and you answer me with a cryptic question that's not very helpful," I fret.

"I'm not trying to confuse you," she responds. "But you're just coming out of a really bad situation. I want you to take it slow. Are you ready to take on another relationship, with Jack Milian of all people?"

"Relationship!" I retort. "I'm just trying to cope with what happened tonight. I'm trying to figure out why Jack kissed me, why he was so affectionate. He's so...different. And you were the one that was all, 'he's got beautiful eyes' and 'he's a good guy,

Ellie,'" I say mockingly. "I'm confused because I liked it, Marie. His arms around me felt safe and comforting, and I need that, I need it so much!"

She peers at me, her eyes narrowed, mulling over my words.

"I know you need it, Ellie, and I'm happy Jack gave you that, because he is different," she says finally. "He's no Mike, that's for sure. He *is* a good egg. Hell, you experienced it yourself tonight. You wouldn't be so confused, if he had been another Mike." She's eyeing me sideways, checking that I'm not sulking at her unflattering inference about my ex. "Mike is a friend, and I care for him, but honestly, he was never this affectionate in comparison. I mean, he loved you, but did he ever show it so openly?"

"There were moments," I reply pensive.

"Moments, Ellie, in three years, just moments," she sighs. "Whatever this thing with Jack turns out to be, whatever *you* want it to turn into, just take it slow. You've had enough heartache for one lifetime. And while Jack may help you heal, there's always a risk. It's part of the deal of life. Just make sure you're ready to handle it. That's all. One step at a time."

"And?" I ask, because I know there's more coming.

"And," she gives me an uneasy look. "On the way here, I was pumping Sam for info on Jack.

He's a hottie, that one, and I've heard he's got women at his beck and call. Sam insinuated that he may be dating someone. I couldn't get a definitive answer out of him, but I thought you should know. I'm not saying he's a player. I'm just saying don't pin all your hopes on him, at least not until you know him better. 'Comforting, safe' arms is a powerful thing, Ellie."

I frown in thought. I am scared of getting hurt again, and I'm trying to understand my feelings for Jack. Do I have feelings for Jack, or is he just a hell of a guy that happened to me one night at a bar when I needed affection? It's certainly too soon to think I have any real feelings for him, but I do like him, and I want to see him again. I can definitely benefit from his kind of affection. And frankly, he's nothing to scowl at!

But the question remains...

Can I put my need for affection before Jack's friendship with Mike? That would be incredibly selfish. I could potentially hurt Jack and get my heart broken all over again. Not to mention that all possibilities of a renewed relationship between Mike and me will surely disappear.

Don't be stupid, Ellie. That possibility is long gone.

"Listen, I don't think Jack's lady conquests or girlfriends are a problem. Frankly, they're none of my concern. I do admit what happened between us was quite...thrilling."

I'm deceiving myself, it was more than that, but my ego has taken over in an attempt to protect me.

"I have no intention of getting into any kind of relationship with him. One, I agree with you, my heart is still healing. Two, Jack is my ex's friend," I assure her.

"Okay, Ellie, if you say so. I just thought I should give you the scoop."

"I know, and I love you for watching out for me," I blow her a kiss, grateful to have a friend who understands me.

"Also," she says as she's about to leave. "Don't be scared of another chance at love, Ellie. Hold steady and accept whatever good things come your way. Give it a chance. If it's with Jack, no other woman can get in the way. Mike shouldn't be an obstacle either. Remember, he left you. You deserve happiness, Ellie. Promise me."

I nod yes and blow her another kiss.

She smiles, winks, and says good night.

CHAPTER 12

Christmas is just around the corner. I can't believe the year is almost over. So much has happened since I moved to LA.

Back then, I had hoped to spend the holidays with Mike and his family. I met his mom last Christmas and gave her a lovely gift. I was looking forward to getting to know my would-be mother-in-law.

How life changes...that premise now seems inane.

We're spending Christmas with Marie's parents in Phoenix. I would have liked to go home to Chicago, but I'm low on cash. I told mom I have a lot of work, and she understood. She's happy knowing I'll be spending the holidays with Marie and her parents, whom are like family.

Despite everything that's happened, my luck continues to change for the better. I heard back from the magazine and have a second interview set for early next year. It's already mid-December, and most people are preparing for some much needed holiday R&R.

And tomorrow is the 18th, my birthday.

This would normally be the perfect excuse to throw a party, something Marie and I excel at, but this year I've opted for a quiet celebration. I've also rejected Marie's suggestion that we go out with Sam and Jack. I'm not quite sure what that night at Busby's was about, and I haven't heard from Jack since. I'm starting to think the player reputation is true, but I don't want to think about it too much.

I'm getting a head start on my first New Year's resolutions: positive thoughts, positive attitude.

❧❧❧

I reach for the iPhone that won't stop ringing, and open one eye to examine it. It's 6:00 a.m., and it's Rob.

"Hi," I answer in a muffled voice.

"It's your birthday, hey, hey, it's your birthday...Ellie's getting *old*, it's her birthday," he sings.

I snort a laugh.

"Happy birthday, I love you!" Then he adds in a

low voice, like someone's watching him, "Have to go, a client just came in."

"I love you too!" I shout back, as he's hanging up.

I yawn with a happy smile, turn to my side, snuggle, and go back to sleep.

I wake up with "Las Mañanitas" blaring all over the house. The iPhone says it's 7:00.

What a great way to wake up!

Marie's in the kitchen in her PJs making coffee, waiting for me with my favorite Triple Berry Short Cake from Sweet Lady Jane. She's the best at spoiling me.

"Happy Birthday!" she greets me with open arms. "Cake and coffee for breakfast?"

"Sounds delicious," I give her a grateful smile, hug her tightly, shaking her from side to side, and don't let go.

"Ah, stop," she laughs.

I let go when my cell pings. My stomach drops, because I'm secretly hoping it's Jack.

Sam: Happy BDay Ellie! Big kiss!

"Sam," I hold up my cell to show Marie, before grabbing some coffee.

"Are you sure you don't want the guys to join us at your birthday dinner tonight?" she places a slice of cake on my plate, as she sits at the table.

I shake my head no.

"You can call or text him, Ellie."

"I don't know what you mean, Marie," I narrow my eyes at her, as I sit at the table and pour half-and-half in my coffee.

"His name is Jack, and he's waiting to hear from you."

"What!" I stop stirring my coffee and stare at her, startled.

"Thought you didn't know what I meant," she teases.

"Seriously, we're going to play this game, on my birthday?"

"I stopped by Trader Joe's last night to get some last minute groceries, and I bumped into Jack. He asked about you. I told him you're doing well, and he said he hopes to see you soon."

"See *me* soon or see *us* soon?" I question dramatically.

"See *you* soon," she points at me, mid-spoonful of cake.

"And you're telling me this just now because...?" I sound more peeved than I intend.

"Because you were sleeping when I got home, and you just woke up, birthday girl."

"Oh," I mope. "It's my birthday, and he should reach out to me. He's got a great excuse. Don't you think?"

"Yes, he should, and yes, he does," she laughs,

shaking her head amused.

Glad I can entertain her.

❧❧❧

Marie and I continue celebrating my birthday with a delicious dinner at Frida Mexican Cuisine in Beverly Hills, one of my favorite restaurants.

My rib-eye tacos are delicious, and Marie sure looks like she's enjoying her ceviche, because she's unusually quiet.

And the drinks are superb!

Between margaritas, we brush up on everything that's happened, including my crushed life plans with Mike and my new friendship with Jack.

"Most of all, Ellie, I'm glad you're almost your old self. I can see it. You're more present, more determined, more alive, and it's great to witness," she observes cheerfully.

"I am better, that's for sure. The responsibilities at the record label, the freelance, and the job search have kept me busy and distracted," I say between sips of my margarita.

"And Jack. He's been quite a distraction," she says suggestively.

I take a big gulp of my drink, because I don't know how much credit to give him. That night at Busby's was a bit of a turning point, but I haven't heard from him since.

And it's been two weeks.

Jack and Ellie could turn out to be more of a complication than Mike and Ellie.

"I do have to admit his attentiveness was surprising, and what I didn't know I needed. But I've just technically met him, and I haven't heard from him. Maybe it's for the best," I try to sound nonchalant.

"But there might be something there, Ellie. He wouldn't have asked about you, if he wasn't interested at least a tiny, tiny bit," she banters.

I grin, hoping she's right, because deep down I do want to see him again.

Then she adds a warning, "Just try not to get hurt. Jack is hot, but you and he becoming a thing has the possibility of creating a brouhaha that can potentially end his friendship with Mike. Dating your best friend's ex...yikes."

"Well, that's disconcerting!"

How did we go from Jack may be interested in you, to you can end his friendship with Mike and fuck up his life?

"Talk about a guilt trip," I add offended.

"No, no, no," she back peddles quickly. "That's not what I mean..."

"I've thought about that too, Marie," I interrupt her. "It was just one kiss, nothing more. And I shouldn't give a crap about what can upset Mike. You said it yourself, he left me. But I don't want

Jack caught in the crossfire of 'Mike and Ellie's bitchy fallout.' He doesn't deserve that, because he's been nothing but kind to me. All I know right now is Jack made me feel...good, despite my injured heart," I say candidly, the margaritas obviously affecting me. "Whatever happens next, I don't know, and right now, I don't care," I giggle.

"I'm not trying to guilt trip you, please know that. That's the last thing I would do. But looking at this from the outside, I can see where the chips have the potential of falling. I don't want you getting tangled up and hurt again. That's all," she takes my hand and squeezes it to reassure me.

"I do know, and I appreciate your honesty. It may burn sometimes, but I know it comes from a place of love. I can't ask for anything more."

I lift my margarita glass as a peace offering, "Cheers!"

I don't want to talk about Jack or Mike anymore. It's my birthday, I'm a year older, hopefully a bit wiser, and I just want to celebrate.

"Damn, I can be bitchy when I'm drinking," she jibes.

"Can't argue with that," I stick my tongue out at her playfully. "Thank you for this dinner, Marie, for getting me out of bed, for supporting me no matter what."

"We're sisters, and you'd do the same for me," she replies, lifts her margarita glass to me and we click, "Salud!"

My iPhone pings.

Jack: Happy birthday beautiful! See you soon yea?

"It's Jack!" I'm giddy with excitement and show Marie my cell.

CHAPTER 13

"Hiya, beautiful!" My bestie Rob twirls me around when he sees me. I've come to pick him up at LAX. He's visiting for Christmas and New Year's.

He just broke up with his girlfriend, and decided to spend the holidays with me to put some distance between her and his injured heart.

I love having him here.

He's tall, athletic, and irreverent, and at 25, he's wise beyond his years. He's very handsome and would be perfect for me, if we hadn't fallen head over heels in friendship first. We joke that we'll marry each other if neither of us finds our true love by the time I'm 35.

I share everything with him, and he always

gives me brutal, honest advice. I can do without the brutal, but the honest I can use, especially now that I'm seeing Jack tomorrow.

"How's what's-her-name?" I ask about his ex.

"I don't know," he says in a low, husky voice and shrugs. "I don't really want to discuss it. It was too short, too fast, and too meaningless. And by that, I mean the relationship," he quips.

"Ha, ha, ha," I retort sarcastically. "I love having you here, Robby Dovey!"

I enjoy tormenting him with my overly silly nickname. He says it's too cutesy, because he's such a jock. I think he secretly loves it, because he's never asked me to stop.

"It's good to see you too, scoundrel. I've missed you," his green eyes dance with joy, as he gives me another big bear hug.

His blond, wavy hair is much longer than the last time I saw him — when he flew me to New York the weekend after I confronted Mike — and it's falling over his face. I reach up and move a few locks of hair away from his eyes.

He smiles sweetly and returns my display of affection. "Mi nena, my *sui generis*, and, oh, so sophisticated diva," he says lovingly, grabs my hand and kisses it gently. He's reminding me of Miguel Bosé's song, "Nena," which he once dedicated to me — though he added a few ornate words to make me blush.

I smile back timidly, as we head out of the airport.

❧ ❧ ❧

"How's the job?" I ask Rob during the drive home. He's a director at a talent agency and knows everyone who's anyone.

"Stressful as always," he sighs, while checking his emails on his iPhone. "We're still spending Christmas in Phoenix?" he looks up at me and puts the device away.

"Yes, Marie's mom and dad are expecting us. They're amazing, and I'm sure we're going to have a great time," I reassure him.

Marie's parents moved to the scorching, hot desert called Phoenix last year. They've always treated me like a second daughter, and they don't mind the mayhem that Marie and I get into during the holidays. In fact, they're usually right there with us, helping to plan and execute the crazy party ideas we come up with. As an only child, they're grateful Marie and I love each other like sisters.

"Hi, gorgeous," Marie welcomes Rob, when we arrive home. "How was your flight?"

"Uneventful," he replies, hugging her.

"Looking good, Mr. All-tall-and-muscular," she examines him.

"I try," he jests.

It's late, and we all head to my bedroom to begin the long catch up.

Rob's lying on the bed next to me, my head is on his chest, and Marie is sitting with her legs crossed near my feet.

"So, I'm meeting the infamous Jack Milian tomorrow?" he asks mischievously.

"Yes," I feign disinterest.

"What's he like, Marie?"

Why does he want to hear it from her and not me?

She giggles, and I sulk.

"He's great, you'll like him," she grins.

"You know I wasn't very keen on Mike, at all!"

"She's aware," I respond.

"Yeah, she told me. Harsh!"

"I was right," he snaps back.

"I'm still here, I can hear you," I say to both of them.

"We know," they counter in unison, laughing.

"Back to Jack, where are we going tomorrow?" he asks.

"Conga Room at LA Live," replies Marie. "Some band Jack wants to see."

"Sam too," I interject, arching an eyebrow.

They laugh again.

At me? I hope not.

"Baby, let's go to the Conga!" says Rob. "I must

meet this Jack, and see if he's man enough for my Ellie."

"Hey," I hit him softly on his abs. "Nothing to check. He's not mine, I'm not his."

"You're not Mike's either," he bluntly reminds me.

Brutal and honest! Sometimes I wish he had a better filter, because the truth sure hurts.

"Sorry, baby girl, but it's true. Please don't hate me," he says softly.

I gaze up at him, brooding. "I can never hate you."

He kisses my hair, making amends. "I know."

૭ઌ ૭ઌ ૭ઌ

"Wheet whew!" whistles Rob when he sees me. "Damn, you're all tall and hot!"

I'm only 5'6" but I'm wearing four-inch heels, and I've gained some of the weight I lost during the Mike-depression era. I'm thrilled, because I got some of my curves back.

"Nice outfit! If this is the Jack effect, I like it!" he eyes me from top to bottom.

I roll my eyes, trying to hide my nervous smile.

I'm wearing a camel colored leatherette midi-tube skirt, a black, sleeveless, one-shoulder top, and open-toe ankle booties.

Teasing smartass! He's seen me in similar

outfits before.

"Ready?" asks Marie. "They're here."

Jack is wearing a steel-blue colored shirt, dark jeans, and that same black leather jacket from the other night.

He's breathtaking.

I make the necessary introductions.

Rob must approve, because he gives me a far too devilish wink. He immediately asserts that he's riding to LA Live with Sam and Marie.

Sneaky devil!

Jack escorts me to his car, his hand on the small of my back, making me feel wanted and safe. My body immediately approves, sending tingles all over me.

ぷぷぷぷ

The Conga Room is less crowded than expected. We make our way to find a table. Jack and Sam head to the bar to fetch our drinks.

They come back with a round of beers. Jack scoots his chair closer to mine, and pulls me in, so close that my arm is resting on his chest. He's holding my hand under the table, and our fingers are intertwined.

I'm getting used to his candid affection. It's new and exciting. But I'm a bit scared, and find myself wondering where this is going and how long it's going to last. The truth is that getting affection without the fear of it being taken away capriciously is new to me. But one look at his gorgeous face, those arresting eyes that look ocean blue thanks to the color of his shirt, and my reservations seem smaller, less important.

The band starts to play, and everyone's attention turns to the stage.

Almost everyone's...

Jack and I are gazing at each other.

"Come," he whispers in my ear, grabs his drink, and leads me to a dark corner of the bar.

He sits on a high stool, facing the stage, and I stand between his legs facing him. He's resting his elbows on top of the bar, still holding my hand. He seems distracted watching the band and drinking his beer, though he occasionally looks at me with a beguiling grin.

He shares his beer with me, like he did at Busby's.

I'm happy to be here, so close to him, taking in his scent.

It's intoxicatingly sexy!

I lean against him, place my idle hand on his chest, and stare at the bartender who's taking a break at the moment.

I can feel his heart beating.

He's not really watching the band. He's trying to control his agitated breathing, as am I. He eventually gives up the fight and kisses my hair. I pull away from him slightly, and we contemplate each other for what seems forever.

He hasn't let go of my hand, and our fingers are intertwined tightly around each other's. They're twisting and pulling again and again, like they're making desperate, eager, fervid love. I don't know how long we do this, minutes, hours...but it's one of the most sensual experiences I've ever had.

The band finishes playing, and he pulls me into him and kisses me sweetly on the cheek.

"They're coming," he breathes in my ear.

I turn around and see Rob is leading the way toward us. I lean into him briefly to let him know I understand, then immediately move away.

"I'm starving. Let's get something to eat," says Rob, as he reaches us and puts his arm around my shoulders. "Hmm, interesting sight," he says, so only I can hear.

I smile timidly at him.

"I got you, sweet girl," he winks and kisses my hair. "Let's head out, people," he shouts above the music, gesturing with his hand.

I nod okay and take a quick peek at Jack, who's grinning.

"After you," Jack gestures to Rob with a wicked smile.

CHAPTER 14

It's a bit chilly outside, and I didn't bring a jacket. Good thing the restaurant options are all within a quick walk.

We decide on Rosa Mexicano for tacos and more beers. We're seated almost immediately. Jack is securely nestled next to me.

We're checking the menu options, when Rob absentmindedly blurts out, "Damn, there are some *hot* ladies out tonight!"

Of course he noticed the many scantily dressed women in and around the LA Live.

Sam and Jack laugh and nod in agreement.

"Welcome to La-La Land," puns Sam.

"Typical boys, so easily distracted," quips Marie, shaking her head in admonishment.

I, on the other hand, find it galling.

How dare they? How dare Jack?

Ugh, he's mine! No, he's not mine, but we just spent hours fondling each other — well, kind of.

"I'm out of here," I babble to myself and abruptly get up to leave.

"Where are you going?" shouts Marie.

"I'm not hungry!" I shout back, without giving them a second glance.

Damn, damn, damn, what am I doing?

My head is spinning from the beers I've already consumed — *Jack's beers.*

I walk toward the Conga Room, but I don't have the slightest idea where I'm going or what I'm doing. I wander through LA Live, until the wooziness gets the best of me.

I'm so dizzy!

I lean against the wall near the Starbucks, my arms folded, and I'm scowling.

What now?

I'm trying to catch my breath and regain my composure. People are staring at me as they pass by, and all I can do is look back at them with a timid smile.

I'm okay, people, move on!

But I'm not okay.

That's quite a scene I just made!

I'm staring at the ground laughing, suddenly realizing how comical my behavior is. I occasionally look up at the people passing by eyeing me.

Then I catch a glimpse of him from the corner of my eye. It's Jack, franticly looking for me.

I keep laughing, as I see him head straight for me. He's in front of me in two seconds, but doesn't say a word. He just grabs me by the waist and pulls me into him forcefully.

Damn, he's strong!

He wraps his arms around me, one hand on my hip, the other in my hair, supporting my head as he kisses me passionately and desperately, like he's been craving me since our first kiss. His needy arms are pressing me to him. My hands move to his hair, fisting it, returning his possession.

No one else exists. It's just him and me, and our lips and tongues in perfect harmony, savoring, biting, and thirsting for each other, like our hands had done earlier.

He stops, breathless, and leans his head against the nape of my neck.

"Are you okay?" he exhales sharply.

I nod yes, my fingers still in his hair, and I kiss the side of his forehead.

"Don't *ever* do that again, Ellie."

"I'm sorry," I reply repentant, but thrilled that he came looking for me.

He looks up and kisses my lips again, a soft, tender kiss. "Crazy girl."

I briefly look at the crowd walking by staring at

us, and see that Sam, Marie, and Rob are searching for us. "They're looking for us," I say quietly, as I'm kissing the side of his lips.

He reluctantly releases me from the tight embrace and takes my hand. "Let's go," he leads, and calls out to them.

Only Rob notices that Jack and I are holding hands. Sam is too busy with Marie to notice anything's happening around him. Rob winks at me and catches up to Sam and Marie, who are now walking ahead of us.

We're heading toward the parking lot.

"We're going home?" I ask.

"We didn't get to eat, with my emergency rescue and all," he mocks.

"I'm sorry," I apologize again, hoping he doesn't hold that rash behavior against me. I don't know what got into me.

He smiles and kisses my hand sweetly.

"Before I came looking for you, I suggested my place. Mario is crashing there for a couple of days, while his apartment gets a new paint job, and he has friends over. I'm sure they have plenty of food and drinks," he explains.

"Mario's at your place right now?" I sound bit more serious than I mean.

"Yes, do you mind going there?"

"No, of course not," I reply, because it's the truth. He can take me to the moon right now, and

I'd gladly go.

"Good," he grins, and we follow our friends to the parking lot.

We're turning the corner toward the street where the parking lot is located, when he abruptly stops. He pulls me into him again to steal another kiss. He pins me tightly around my waist, his lips savoring mine, his tongue playing with mine.

It's mind-altering.

He's deliciously inebriating.

"Mmm," he grunts, as he releases me slightly. "Ellie," he whispers against my lips, kissing me again softly.

I'm breathing heavily, euphoric at what he can do to me. In the brief time I've known him, he's been able to make me feel safe, adored, and protected, all at once. He's so affectionate and passionate. It's confounding how he doesn't hold back.

Why didn't I find him first?

"Come," he kisses me softly on the cheek. "Let's catch up to the others, before they come looking for us again," he smiles and walks forcefully, pulling at my hand.

I follow him beaming, on my own enraptured cloud nine, where only he and I exist.

CHAPTER 15

"Honey, I'm home," jokes Jack, as he's opening the door to his apartment.

It's quite a large place, a modern and open loft near the beach in Venice.

Jack is doing quite well for himself.

"Welcome home," replies Mario with open arms. He's smiling, until he realizes Jack's not alone. "Hey," he quickly alters his greeting and glowers at Jack.

"Come, baby," Jack leads me to a slate-gray, plush sofa in the living room, after he's made the necessary introductions.

Baby? I like the sound of that!

Sam and Marie sit on a sofa opposite us and cuddle, while Rob follows Mario to the kitchen to check out the food and drink options.

"Well, there's lots of pizza, pizza and pizza," exclaims Rob amused.

"And to drink?" asks Jack.

"The choices are slightly better...beer, vodka, tequila, rum. What would you like?"

"Whatever my baby wants," says Jack and kisses me on the lips for everyone to see.

I'm grinning at him, completely infatuated. It takes me a second to notice the chaos around us has abruptly stopped.

Sam's blatantly staring, his mouth silently saying, "What?!"

Marie is grinning fervently, as is Rob.

Mario's standing behind us like a statue, open mouthed, holding a bottle of rum, while his friends are gawking at us.

Why?

Then it hits me. They all know Mike. They all know our history, and they're all wondering what the hell is going on between Jack and me.

"Whatever she wants, we'll share," repeats Jack, ignoring their stares and kisses me again, this time longer and deeper.

He's making sure everyone knows that first kiss was not a mistake, he is with me, and he doesn't care whether they approve or not.

He's claiming me, end of story!

Everyone scatters back to their drinks and

conversations.

Except Sam.

He's still staring, frowning, wondering how and when Jack and I happened.

Marie whispers something in his ear, and he finally looks away, appeased by whatever she said to him.

ৡৡৡ

Jack is embracing me firmly by the front door. We just got home from his place, and it's late. Neither of us wants the night to end.

Marie walks past us and simply waves good night. Rob follows her but stops near us for a second to gawk.

Marie turns back and grabs him by the shirt. "Come on, this is none of your business," she pulls at him.

He laughs and follows her inside, leaving Jack and me embracing.

I don't know why we don't head inside, but I think it's because we don't want to let go of each other for one second.

"What are you doing for Christmas?" he asks, nibbling at my ear lobe.

I feel my entire body shiver, but I manage to reply, "We'll be in Phoenix, at Marie's parents. We're driving there in the morning. What are you doing for New Year's?"

His mouth is making its way down my neck, to my clavicle, and my chest. His vigorous lips are slowly replying to my question, as he plants soft kisses along the way.

"I'm heading to San Francisco with my family. The trip's been on the books for months."

"Mmm," I moan, feeling a warm flood surging through my body.

Damn, he's good at this!

"We'll be here," I reply in a high-pitched voice thanks to his oral skills.

He stops his adulation just enough to gaze into my eyes, "I'll miss you."

I grin at him, take his beautiful face with my hands, and kiss him gently, "Me too."

He tightens his hold on me, pressing me into him so I can feel his erection. He kisses me, deliciously pulling at my lips, biting and sucking.

"Mmm," I moan again, as his lips move to my neck, nibbling at it.

I'm trembling in his arms.

"You're mouthwatering, Ellie. You have the softest skin," he babbles, crushing me into him with his arm, while his other hand travels to my breast. He pulls down the side of my top, which easily gives way, and he gets easy access to his goal. His lips continue a downward path through my collarbone until he reaches my breast. He finds my nipple and kisses it, pulls at it, and suckles.

My eyes are closed and my hands are in his hair, fisting it tightly, holding him in place. I'm biting my lower lip, lost in the exquisite feeling of his mouth on me as he suckles, and a blaze of pure pleasure surges through me. My mind is cloudy, lost in our tryst. But I open my eyes for a second and realize where we are.

"Jack, we're outside!" I say dismayed and self-conscious.

"Fuck!" he stops, quickly fixes my top, and hugs me tightly. He kisses my cheek tenderly, as if saying he's sorry he lost control.

"If you weren't leaving in the morning," he whispers suggestively in my ear, pushing his bulging erection into me.

"I know. I wish I wasn't." I'm barely keeping my wits about me.

We're holding each other, our hearts pounding with carnal desire, which sadly will not be satisfied tonight.

I want him. I want him badly.

This gorgeous, sexy man does things to me, rare, unique things deep inside. How is all this allure and magnetism packed inside one man?

And he wants me. It's mind blowing.

But I'm torn about us, especially when I inconveniently remember Marie's words, *"Dating your best friend's ex...yikes."*

Maybe it's a blessing that our wanton desires have been thwarted for tonight. We need more time to figure this out.

"I better go," he says softly.

"No," I pucker and kiss the side of his lips, then pull at his succulent lower lip.

He tastes so good! I can stay here forever.

"I don't want to go, but you're getting up early to get on the road. You should sleep. Please don't drive if you're not well-rested, promise me."

"I won't," I promise him, still pouting because he's leaving.

"I love it when you pout. You make me want to do this," he pulls at my lower lip with his lips. "Mmm," he groans, before releasing it, and then spanks my behind, making me yelp.

"Night, baby," he smacks a loud, playful kiss on my lips, before letting go of me.

I wave him goodbye and miss him already.

❧❧❧

I didn't sleep much after Jack left. I was lost in daydreams of our amazing night together, and our illicit and brazen tryst outside.

We were up so early to get on the road, that I only got a couple of hours of sleep.

Rob is taking the first turn driving, and Marie is riding shotgun.

I'm happy in the back seat of Marie's red Toyota Prius, trying to finally get some shuteye. If I could just get Jack out of my mind...his touch, his hands, the coarseness of his barely-there stubble sanding my soft skin as his mouth traveled down to my breast...mmm...his suckling. The taste of his lips, his mouth!

"What's that salacious little grin about?" teases Marie.

I open my eyes and see her staring at me, amused.

"I don't know what you mean," I grin back and close my eyes, hoping her curiosity ceases.

"Oh, please, that's one wicked, *wicked* little smile if I've ever seen one."

"Yeah, Ellie," chimes Rob, trying to catch a glimpse of me through the rearview mirror.

"Hmm, nothing," I say and keep my eyes closed. I don't tell them about the racy episode with Jack last night.

That one is just for me.

CHAPTER 16

It's Christmas Eve morning. Marie and I are busy helping her mom, Sofia, prepare the turkey and side dishes — we always celebrate on the 24th, as is the custom in Latino culture.

Even Rob is busy, helping Marie's dad, Eddie, stock the outdoor bar with an assortment of liquor, juices, beer, and ice to keep us cocktail-happy throughout the night.

The Albas' home is a three-bedroom ranch style house. The kitchen-dining-living room area is one open space, which makes the home seem larger. The living room faces a large patio area that features a pool, a couple of trees and a lounging area with large, plush sofas.

Dinner will happen inside, but after-midnight

cocktails and the gift exchange will most certainly be outside by the pool. Thankfully, the night should provide a break from this intense heat.

The Albas have invited several of their friends to join us, mostly couples whose children are not coming home for Christmas. We're expecting a long, cheerful night.

"I'm so glad you made it down. I was afraid you'd decide to stay in LA," says Sofia, as we're helping to set the dining room table.

"We'd never do that, mom," counters Marie.

"Honey, you know we support whatever you do. We don't want to impose. You girls are young and have a lot of living to do. By the way, Ellie, how's Mike?"

Marie glowers at her.

"Oh, did I say something wrong?" she asks, concerned she just put her foot in her mouth.

"No, not at all. Mike and I aren't seeing each other anymore," I explain, trying not to make a big deal out of this news.

"Oh, honey, I'm sorry. I didn't mean to make you sad," she responds.

"You didn't make me sad, Sofie," I reply with a soft smile.

I've called her Sofie since I first met her at age 5. When I respectfully called her *Mrs. Alba*, she responded gingerly, "How polite, sweet, sweet girl. Call me Sofie."

"My mom asked about him too, when we FaceTimed earlier. I should've disclosed that information before, but it's old news, and it just slipped my mind," I say casually, hoping this will end all conversations about Mike.

"I remember how hard a breakup can be," Sofie tries to console me.

"Mom!" Marie stares daggers at her.

"I'm just saying I was once young too, and I did date other men before your dad," she continues, despite Marie's glare.

"Mom, stop!" Marie is mortified at her mom's candid observations.

I smile at their exchange. They're so much alike, even if Marie doesn't want to admit it.

"Sweetheart, did Sara and Mateo get the gifts we sent?" Sofie asks me.

"Yes, and they asked me to thank you very much. I told them you had received theirs. They're very grateful I'm spending Christmas with you," I reply with a smile.

"We wouldn't have it any other way. We love you like a daughter."

Her kind words get to me, and I'm starting to tear up with nostalgia of home. I do miss mom and dad.

Eddie notices and suggests a toast. He quickly fills some glasses with wine and hands them to us. "Here's to always enjoying a great Christmas Eve with family and friends. Salud!"

We all click glasses, and he gives me a kind smile and a wink.

❧❧❧❧

I'm staring at the ceiling unable to sleep. I'm in a food coma from the excessive amount of food and drinks I've consumed. Christmas is one of the holidays I consider free-zones, meaning no worrying about counting calories or carbs.

It was a marvelous night, with lovely older people giving us young ones a lot of advice. Not too long ago, I would've dismissed their words, but today, I was taking notes, especially when sweet Alice came up with things like, "Life's too short to sit around crying over spilled milk. Pick up the glass, clean up the spill, and get yourself another serving."

Hear, hear Alice!

I'm cleaning up my messy past, and Jack is helping me.

"Jack," I sigh his name quietly, smiling remembering his text exactly at midnight.

Jack: Merry Christmas baby. I miss you really miss you! I owe you so many kisses!

I close my eyes and fall asleep content.

Mike is holding me with one arm around my waist, as we dance at the New Year's party. It's an upbeat song we both love, and he's holding me tightly.

He's so cocky, and I'm bewitched. He rules his world, and I can't get enough.

"Happy New Year!" we hear people scream above the music.

We stop dancing, and he presses me into him with both arms.

"Happy New Year," I whisper in his ear, and he rewards me with a radiant smile.

"Happy 2012," he says and kisses me on the lips.

"Happy 2013," I say and kiss him back, because I'm hoping to spend many New Year's to come with him.

"Happy 2014," he replies following my lead, and we kiss again.

"Happy 2015," we say in unison smiling, and we kiss one more time.

I'm starting 2012 with this hot guy, and I'm the happiest girl here.

"Shit!" I wake with a start, my heart pounding out of my chest. I'm sweating, literally sweating, and the AC is on full blast.

"Ellie, are you okay?" Marie asks half asleep.

I've woken her up. We're sharing sleeping

quarters, so Rob could take the spare bedroom.

I sit up on the guest bed, rub my face, and fan my cami. "I was dreaming. Sorry I woke you."

Marie sits up as well, "A nightmare?"

"Yes...no. I was dreaming of Mike, when we first hooked up, New Year's 2012. We kissed each other once for every New Year up to 2015. I don't know why we stopped there."

"Why are you dreaming with Mike?"

"No idea. I was thinking of Jack when I fell asleep."

"Don't read too much into it. Don't let it mess with your psyche. Go back to sleep, dream of Jack," she yawns, lies back on the bed, and quickly falls back to sleep.

I close my eyes intent on dreaming of Jack, but it's Mike who invades my subconscious again.

"I mean look at you, such a beautiful girl next to me. How did I get you?" He's examining me with reverence.

We're sitting in his car, outside a restaurant where we just had dinner. He's extra attentive tonight, and I'm giddy.

"Muah!" he kisses me loudly on my ear, making me squeal like a little girl.

"What's that for?" I giggle.

"Just because," he gazes into my eyes, grinning. "One day, when we get married," he

proceeds, and my world stops.

"Yes?" I say, with a coy smile.

"One day, in about five years or so, we'll get married, and it's going to be fantastic!"

Hearing those words come out of his lovely mouth makes my heart swell so much, it almost hurts.

"What the hell!" I mumble to myself, as I wake up again, startled by my irreverent dreams.

I'm careful not to wake Marie again and head to the kitchen for a glass of water. The house is quiet and dark, so I use the light from my iPhone to guide my steps.

The ice-cold water cools me off and helps bring my heart rate down.

I'm so tired, but I don't want to go back to sleep, back to dreaming of Mike. I contemplate heading to the patio and staring up at the stars until morning comes. I decide against it, because I'll end up scrutinizing those troubling dreams, and I'll look miserable in the morning.

I head back to the bedroom, pondering if Jack is sleeping soundly, maybe dreaming of me.

I could only hope.

After what seems like hours, I fall back into a dreamless sleep.

CHAPTER 17

We say our goodbyes to Marie's parents and begin our drive back to LA. Rob is behind the wheel again, and I'm riding shotgun this time. But I'm pensive, and Rob can't take my silence anymore.

"I need a talker next to me when I drive, Ellie, a distraction to keep me awake. It's a long, lonely drive so entertain me, or I'm going to wake up Marie and send you to the back seat."

"Geez, Robby Dovey, take it down a notch," I tickle him, and he chuckles.

"Fine," he grins lovingly.

He can never stay mad at me.

"But spill it. What are you so preoccupied with?"

I tell him about my dreams, and how I woke up bewildered. I don't want to obsess about the past anymore, but those dreams were so vivid.

Rob hears me out as I'm going in circles, questioning everything, my mood, my actions, my wants, my fears, and doubts. It seems hours pass, and I'm still rehashing the same subjects.

"Rob, aren't you going to say anything?"

"No, Ellie," he replies sternly. "You already know the answer to every single question and doubt. People change, things change, and Mike didn't choose you. I'm here for you, to listen all day and all night, at least until I leave. So talk as much as you want. I will listen, because I love you. I can do that for you, but don't expect me to help you rationalize why you should go back to being hung up on Mike. I mean, who gets lucky enough to stumble onto someone like Jack? Only you, Ellie, and that's because despite your lapse in judgment with Mike, you are a loving, wonderful person, and you deserve a 'Jack.' So stop with Mike already. For fuck's sake, get out of your own way, Ellie. Please!"

I stare out the window and muse. He's right. Dreams are just old memories. Mike is out of my life, as it should be. Jack is my present. He's shown me another side of love.

Do I want to risk that? Of course not!

"I'm not stuck on Mike, and I'm not choosing him," I defend myself, without looking at him. "I was just sharing, but I'm done."

He grabs my hand in kisses it, as if saying he's sorry for being so harsh. He pulls at it several times, until I turn to look at him.

"I'm sorry, I love you," he mouths and kisses my hand again.

I smile and turn on the radio. I close my eyes, rest my head on the headrest, and take in the lyrics of the song that's playing, "Stressed Out" by Twenty One Pilots.

I hear Marie softly humming the song from the back seat, making me smile again.

Rob doesn't let go of my hand for hours.

ॐॐॐ

Rob is back in New York. We welcomed 2016 at a VIP event hosted by one of his friends. While it was the most fun I've had in a long time, I was wishing Jack was with me.

By the time we arrived back in LA from Phoenix, he had already left for San Francisco. What comforts me is our constant communication. He texts me these little sweet nuggets of affection that always put a smile on my face and make me feel special.

Jack: Wish you were here
Jack: I'm dying to kiss you
Jack: Thinking of you baby your soft skin your lips

Jack: I can't wait to see you and kiss you
Jack: You were in my dreams last night. I miss you
Jack: 🌑🌑🌑 can't wait to give you these in person

And his text exactly at midnight was the perfect way to ring in the New Year.

Jack: Happy 2016 baby I wish you were here to welcome the year together. Miss you!

But I haven't seen him, and it's mid-January. Unexpectedly, I've been incredibly busy at the record label. We have multiple projects to be released before the end of the first quarter, and I've been working longer hours. I'm more than willing, because it increases my pay, and the experience I'm gaining is invaluable. But I get home so late, and I'm frustrated that Jack and I haven't been able to coordinate a night to see each other.

I'm also wondering if he's seeing someone else. Marie never found out if he is dating someone. Sam isn't forthcoming with any information, as much as Marie has insisted. I almost don't care, because we're just beginning a friendship that I'm hoping will lead to a real relationship. We're not there yet, so I don't have a right to question him.

I'm single, that's very clear to him. If he wants to be with me, he will have to cut ties with whomever he's dating. That's on him.

And thanks to my lucky stars, today I don't have

much time to spend mulling over it. I'm preoccupied preparing for a follow up interview I have tomorrow for the editor position I'm going after.

Jack knows about it and is just as supportive and reassuring as I expected.

Jack: Good luck with your interview tomorrow baby
Ellie: Thank you! 😊
Jack: You got this
Ellie: I hope so
Jack: Know so
Ellie: 😄 Yes
Jack: Do you miss me?
Ellie: No
Jack: 😳
Ellie: Do you miss me?
Jack: Yes
Ellie: That's all that matters! 😁
Jack: Funny!
Ellie: I miss you so much... 😘😘😘
Jack: I need those kisses in person
Ellie: Come get them
Jack: Don't tempt me cause I will
Ellie: I want you to
Jack: Ellie...
Ellie: Jack...
Jack: I'll drop everything and go!
Ellie: Taking a day off, are you?
Jack: LOL! I'm in the middle of negotiating a deal
Ellie: Big shot! What are you doing texting me?
Jack: I always have time for you
Ellie: I should let you go
Jack: No. I'll leave and go see you
Ellie: You can't but I love that you want to
Jack: For you I can and I will

Ellie: You're so damn cute
Jack: Am I?
Ellie: Damn right!
Jack: LOL! You're pretty hot yourself
Ellie: Am I? 🐱
Jack: LOL! Can't wait to touch you again
Ellie: Me too!
Jack: Then let me come to you
Ellie: I'm aching to see you but you're in the middle
    of something important
Jack: I'd drop everything to see you
Ellie: I know and you have no idea how much that
    makes me happy 😘😘😘
Jack: Mmm yummy kisses
Ellie: 💜💜💜 Thank you for your support for always
    cheering me on 😍
Ellie: Now kick some business ass! 💜 xoxo
Jack: You got it baby! xoxo

Geez, this man is incredible! What planet did he come from? We, earthly women, need more like him.

CHAPTER 18

Marie got a promotion. It's quite an accomplishment. She's been at the ad agency just over a year and has proven herself invaluable. Being bilingual, she's the agency's most valuable asset.

We're throwing a backyard party this weekend to celebrate her much deserved good fortune and the fact that my job interview went really well. We've done these shindigs often enough to know exactly what we need to transform the backyard into an LA hotspot within a matter of days.

Sam is helping, of course. He's our designated gofer and handy man to set the patio space to our standards. He's helping us set up the high cocktail tables and chairs we rented, and hang the suspended lights that stretch from one side of the backyard to the other.

Jack offered to help as well, but I turned him down. He's tied up with the opening of two more coffee shops. He's overworked as it is, and I don't want to distract him. He didn't sound too pleased when I rejected his offer, but I know deep inside he's grateful I took his needs into consideration.

We've also hired a bartender for the night. And thanks to Sam, who works for a beer distributer, all the beer is on him. We've also bought an impressive assortment of liquor and plenty of appetizers to feed our guests. Tony, Marie's buddy from the ad agency, has mad music mixing skills and has offered to DJ.

ॐॐॐ

The e-vite went out a few days ago, and we're expecting a very large turnout.

We want everyone to get home safely and have posted an Uber reminder on the bathroom door, with a warning that we reserve the right to hide car keys if anyone insists on driving home drunk. A warning is a warning!

By 8:00 p.m., almost everyone has arrived, and the party is on!

I'm holding a bottle of tequila that I'm taking to the bartender, when I turn and see Mike walking in with four of his friends, including Mario.

What is HE doing here?

I start to panic and look everywhere for Marie, to ask her who invited him. I can't find her, but I'm sure she knows why he's here.

He finds the perfect spot at the entrance of the patio, where he can be as far away from me as possible.

Of course.

He's in my house — for all intents and purposes it is my house — and he still won't even say hello.

He's such an ass, as Rob would say.

I finally see Marie standing by the back entrance to the kitchen.

"You're going to drink that by yourself, muñe?" she teases.

Shit, I'm still holding the bottle of tequila.

I drag her inside the kitchen, where Mike can't see us, and begin to drill her.

"Eh, I invited him. Sorry! Sam kind of mentioned it to him, and he technically is still a friend. I felt obligated," she puts her hands together in prayer in front of her face, hoping I won't be too peeved.

"Well, he didn't even bother to say hello, and I'm one of the hosts. Whatever!" I walk away a bit annoyed, though not at Marie but at myself.

Despite his belligerence, seeing him stirs something inside me. It's something that scares me. He's the ultimate reminder of the pain I've gone through and of how shattered my heart was.

It disturbs my peace of mind.

I'm now anxious at my own party.

I head to the bar and drop off the bottle of tequila I've been holding.

I see Mike again. He's still hanging around the same spot, near the door that leads to the street.

Of course he loiters near the closest possible exit.

He also has an incredible vantage point, and can see me perfectly no matter where I walk to or stand. It's unnerving. I can feel his eyes following me, and I find myself looking back at him.

Damn!

I'm greeting a couple of the guests that just arrived, when I'm suddenly startled by someone's arm wrapping around my waist from behind.

I turn slightly and see Jack sweetly smiling at me. But instead of throwing my arms around him, like I've been aching to do, I unwrap myself from his embrace and harshly step away frowning at him, as if he's a stranger who has no right to touch me.

He glares at me bewildered and confused.

What have I done!

I want to hold him, tell him I'm sorry, but I'm paralyzed. His wounded eyes halt me in place. He's been rejected and dismissed...by me!

He's baffled and humiliated.

Sam is near Mike — he must've arrived with Jack — and he's glaring at me, pissed at my dismissal of his friend.

Mike is scowling at Jack, as if he just committed a mortal sin.

It's like I'm having an out-of-body experience, where a crazed Ellie is hurting Jack, and I can't stop her. I'm in shock and can't move a muscle.

I hurt Jack unintentionally. I did to him what Mike has done to me so many times. I've slain him, the way Mike's acrimonious behavior has slain me over and over.

Jack recovers, his expression now shifting to disappointment. He quickly turns away from me and walks toward Sam and Mike.

I'm frozen in place when Marie finds me.

"What the hell, Ellie, you're pale like a ghost," she says, concerned at the sight of me.

I look at her with horror in my eyes. She grabs me and shakes me. "Shit, Ellie, what happened?"

I recount what I just did, and she pulls me by the hand away from the guys' line of sight.

"Why'd you do that, Ellie? Do you still want Mike?"

"No! I'm a moron!" It's the only explanation I can come up with. My brain is rebooting after a massive system crash.

"Do you want to fix this?" she asks alarmed.

I nod yes, lost in self-anger and confusion.

"Then go throw your arms around him, kiss him, and tell him he just startled you," she advises.

I nod yes, because I can't seem to form any words. She grabs my hand and leads me to find Jack, but as soon as we spot him, we stop in our tracks.

He's standing face to face with Mike, and Mike is berating him. Mike's hands are at his side, but he doesn't need them. His mouth is doing all the damage.

Jack is listening to him, meeting his shrill stare, his hands in his jeans' pockets, and he's absorbing every single crap-filled lexicon Mike is spewing.

I don't think I can feel any worse for what I've done, until Jack turns his head and stares straight at me, still listening to Mike. His eyes are filled with disillusionment, and it pains me, because I'm responsible for it.

Mike's face is so close to Jack's he can almost touch him, and he's going at him, hard!

Mike has no right to interfere or recriminate, but I suspect that's exactly what he's doing. I gave him the green light, when I pushed Jack away. I basically told Mike he can control me, that he can have me back any time he wants, and I will always belong to him.

That one simple, unthinkable, stupid move has undone what Jack and I were building. The trust, the kindness, the love — *yes, the love* — are all gone, because I panicked, because I let my fear of getting hurt again get the best of me and turn me into a raging idiot.

Jack's gaze is still fixated on me, his dejected eyes confirming my fears. Mike is staking his claim...a claim he's no longer entitled to. But the second I brushed-off Jack, I gave him the ammunition he needed.

"Damn, I wish I could hear what Mike is saying to him. I'll ask Sam later," scoffs Marie.

"He won't tell you," I reply with a knot in my throat.

I know he won't, no matter how much he likes Marie. Their friendship is first and foremost, and they will never betray each other's confidence.

When Mike is finally done, Jack turns his head back to look at him for a second, then just leaves.

"Where is he going?" Marie asks panicked.

"I've lost him," is my only reply.

I'm devastated and pissed, pissed at myself.

Jack is the best thing that's happened to me in forever, and I've lost him because deep inside I'm afraid of opening my heart to him, of allowing him to love me.

That's why you've been dreaming of Mike and not Jack!

"What do I do, Marie?"

"Do you want Jack back?"

"Yes," my voice is trembling, because despite my fears, I do love him. He's affectionate, caring and kind. He makes me a better person. I'm a damn fool if I let him go, if I don't tell him how much I care for him, if I don't tell him how sorry I am.

"But I don't deserve him," I say out loud and let out a quiet sob.

"What the hell does that say about you, Ellie? That you sabotaged this amazing thing with Jack because you think you don't deserve him, because you think you're not good enough for him. Think about that for a second. You know better, Ellie. You do!" she scolds.

I'm trying to hold back my tears. She may be right, but I've already ruined everything.

"Call him, text him, find him. And don't let Mike see you like this. Don't give him the pleasure," she urges.

I nod okay and head to my bedroom to try to reach Jack.

જ~જ~જ

My calls are going straight to voicemail. He's either turned off his cell or is rejecting my calls.

Ellie: Jack please call me

I sit on my bed, staring at my iPhone, but I

don't expect him to get back to me, not really.

I hurt him.

He hates me right now.

I hate myself.

I wait, wait and wait...and there's no response after half an hour.

I text him again.

Ellie: Jack please
Ellie: Call me, text me back I need to talk to you
Ellie: Let me explain

I keep waiting, but he doesn't respond.

Tears are rolling down my face when Marie walks in.

"No answer?" she asks concerned.

I shake my head no.

"He'll answer, give him some time. Come join the party, but fix your makeup first. Put on your best smile, and don't let Mike see he's hurt you again."

"No, Marie, this time I hurt myself. I did this."

"Fine, but you can fix it. Just give Jack some time."

"What if that isn't enough?" My voice is shaking, the panic taking hold of me.

"He will talk to you, Ellie, I promise," she tries to console me.

"You think so?"

"Yes. But it may not happen tonight, muñe.

Give him time." She extends her hand to me, but I don't take it.

"I'll be down in a few," I sob.

She reluctantly leaves, and I text Jack one last time.

Ellie: Please don't hate me

I've calmed down enough to start reapplying my makeup, when I hear a ping. I grab my iPhone immediately.

Jack: I don't hate you
Ellie: Why did you leave? Please come back
Jack: I have things to do
Ellie: Ok but please come back
Jack: See you later

He's done with me, and I deserve it!

The tears start flowing again and ruin the freshly applied makeup.

I don't care.

I just want to get this awful guilty feeling out of me.

I sit on my bed and cry, until I can convince myself I can find a way to fix this royal fuckup.

❧❧❧❧

I have on my best fake smile, as I walk around the

party serving drinks. I've become the unofficial bartender, because offering our guests shots of tequila is the best I can do right now — and I'm definitely taking a few myself.

Alcohol makes me either very happy or very sad, and tonight I've decided on happy. I have to keep my spirits up. If I allow myself to believe I've ruined things with Jack for good, I will not be able to live with myself. And I won't let Mike see me sad. He doesn't deserve that much attention.

By midnight, half of our guests are gone, and the rest of us move the party inside. Mike, Sam, Mario, and two of their buddies are still here, as content and comfortable as if they were the guests of honor. I'm starting to resent their presence, but I'm being unfair because they have nothing to do with my mistake. It was all me.

About ten of us are left by 2:00 a.m. Our DJ, Tony, is calling it a night, but he leaves a playlist on my Mac to keep the music going for at least another hour.

I'm making another round of tequila shots, as Mariah Carey's "Without You" starts playing.

Tony has a thing for the classics...

I absentmindedly start singing it to myself.

"Beautiful!" I hear Mike say.

From the corner of my eye, I see his buddies staring at me, and one says, "Yes, she is."

Mike chuckles and replies, "I meant the song."

Bastard! He's playing a cruel game, and I'm his pawn. Well, no more!

ஐஐஐ

Mike hasn't said a word to me the entire night and has kept his distance, as is his modus operandi.

I don't know why he's still here, and I really don't know why he was so rude to Jack, if he wants nothing to do with me. Does he want me back? He'd certainly be failing, if that was his intention. His approach is very questionable.

It's just Mike being Mike.

But my behavior tonight is the most reprehensible. I accept it, I hurt Jack. That's solely on me. It was the last thing I wanted to do, and the first thing I did.

By 3:00, I leave Marie at the party alone with the last few guests still here.

I've had enough.

CHAPTER 19

It's been two months, two long months since Marie's promotion party.

I've begun to take real responsibility for my part in the drama with Mike. I may not have been the one to hurt him or leave him, but I did abandon myself.

Mike is not responsible for that. I am.

I can't continue to blame him for how damaged I've become. I did that all on my own. I allowed myself to sink so low that I couldn't even stand up for myself or defend my feelings for Jack.

Jack's still not speaking to me, not really. He's not rude, but his answers to my texts consist of "yes," "no," and "maybe."

Not exactly a conversation.

"Women love Jack!" Mike's comment haunts me from time to time.

I wonder if he's moved on. As much as it pains me, I wouldn't blame him after the way I've treated him.

I'm losing my mind, feeling dreadful for hurting him. He has every reason to dislike me, if not hate me. I'm desperate to repair the damage, but I've come to the conclusion that I have to fix myself first.

The universe must've heard me, because I stumbled on to a book called *The Silva Mind Control Method* by José Silva. The title initially freaked me out, but after reading the summary and people's reviews, I knew it was exactly what I needed.

I dove into it and finished it in one day.

The Silva Method teaches techniques, through meditation, that give us the ability to create a better life for ourselves. This is exactly what I've been searching for, and I want more.

The book includes information on in-person training seminars. There are Silva professionals teaching the methods all over the world, and I've located a class in Anaheim. It's a bit of a drive from Culver City, but so worth it. Marie is lending me her car.

I'm doing this for me, for my own personal growth. I'm doing this because I'm tired of repeating the same pattern, of being scared of moving on. I'm exhausted with myself for making the wrong choices, and I'm ready to discover a better me.

It's a weekend course, and I start tomorrow morning. I'll be taking the first step toward building a better me. I'm very excited.

࿐࿐࿐

I've barely seen Marie. She's been working incredibly long hours since her promotion, and she gets home with just enough energy to prepare for the next day and then go to sleep. And I was gone last weekend taking the Silva seminar.

Today, we'll finally have a couple of hours to catch up. She called to say she'd be home by 6:00 p.m., and I'm going to surprise her with Thai food, her favorite. I ordered it from a restaurant we both love, because I can't cook to save my life.

"Thank you for ordering Thai," she smiles.

We're sitting on the floor in the living room, having dinner on the coffee table, as usual.

"You're welcome. I would've cooked, but..." I shrug.

"That's okay," she laughs, crunching her nose and shaking her head. She's tried my attempts at cooking before and surely prefers not to do it again.

"How was the Silva training?" she pours a glass of wine for each of us.

"Hmm, transformative. All those techniques in the book came alive. I now have tangible resources at my disposal."

She's eating, listening closely.

"I'm not saying I can fix the entire world, but I can make my life better, and in the process, try to help others. It all starts with me...with us essentially. We decide how we process the positive and negative things that happen to us, whether we hold on to them or let them go, and the impact they have on us," I explain while sipping my wine.

"In theory, I already knew this. I think we all know it to some extent. But how we go from just knowing it, to actually believing it deep inside where it matters, and having the tools to make the positive thoughts work for our benefit, is the rub. How many times have you told me to love myself? And I heard you. I thought I did love myself. But that inner part of me, deep inside where it all starts was like, 'Fool, I don't love you. Why should I? You're not good enough!' Now I have a road map, per se, a direct line to that inner me, to speak to her and show her how to love herself, how to help herself, and how to let go of negativity and fear, so that my conscious self, the me that walks, talks, and lives can thrive in that truth.

"I realized I held on to Mike by choice. I dwelled on the breakup, and damn I was great at it. It was a choice, as horrible as that sounds. Yes, I had to mourn the loss. Yes, I had to feel the pain, but I took it to new heights and prolonged it by choice. Basically, I was afraid, because if he didn't love me, who would? If he didn't see me, who would? If I wasn't good enough for him, who would I be good enough for? At some point, I was only in love with the idea of us. I couldn't let go, because if I did, it would mean that I *was* worthless — as erroneous as that is. So when Jack came along, offering me his heart full of love, I didn't know how to accept it, not entirely. What do I do? I put up a precautionary wall of fear."

Marie's intensely staring at me, frowning, but I don't stop.

"The problem isn't Mike. The problem is how I feel, or *felt* rather, about myself. And by that, I mean it's not his problem that I *had* an addiction to him. It's mine. It's not his responsibility to make me feel good enough, it's mine. Of course I'm good enough, damn it!" I exclaim, sure of myself.

"When Rob asked me why I loved Mike, I didn't have a concrete answer. I always felt like I had to beg for his love. So, why did I love him? Someone can either love us or not. That's on them. It's up to us if we accept a warped kind of love, with those limitations," I continue my confession.

"There are so many things I have to work on, believe me. This isn't magic. But right now, I can actually see things from a better perspective. I can place them in the category where they belong, and let go of what needs to be left behind. I see myself and love myself enough to know that it's okay to make mistakes. It's okay to stumble, and it's okay to move on. It's okay to let go, and it's okay love again, certainly Jack. And most of all, I can survive if I get hurt again," I finally shut up and start eating my food.

Marie's still glaring at me, with her mouth open. Her spoon is suspended mid-way to her mouth. I don't know how long she's been in that position listening to my passionate tale. Did she get all that, or am I going to have to repeat it, because I'm not sure I can remember it all?

"Well, shit, you just fucking blew my mind!" she finally says.

"Right!" I respond, and we both laugh. "I highly recommend you take the seminar too."

"I definitely will, after all that," she agrees and continues eating.

"And speaking of fixing things," I say. "I have to make amends with Jack, even if he wants nothing more to do with me romantically. I owe him an explanation. He has to know that I didn't react to him in that horrible manner because I'm still interested in Mike, but because seeing him reminded me of the devastating pain my heart once felt. I'm working on letting go of that, precisely thanks to *him*. Because he is..." I sigh.

"He is love."

"Then you're going to fight for him?" she asks.

"Oh, hell yes! I hope he'll give me a second chance. He has such a beautiful heart, and that's an amazing prize for the lucky bitch that gets him. Even if he ends up with someone else, I'd root for her, because you have to be thrilled for anyone that wins the lottery with someone like him. But I'm going to do whatever I can to make things right."

"You'd really cheer her on?" she's giving me a wry look.

"Eh...maybe not," I giggle. "But I'm trying to be benevolent here, work with me." We both laugh.

"Since you're on this path of self-discovery, I recommend your next read be *The Power of Now* by Eckhart Tolle," she suggests. "I think you'll find it very interesting. It's on my iPad, if you want to read it."

"I'll start tomorrow," I smile, and we finish our dinner.

CHAPTER 20

I might see Jack tonight. If I do, I'm glad I have a clearer head and heart. A sane, healthy me will make a better apology. I'll do everything I can to explain myself, to share my true feelings with him, and maybe he'll trust me again, maybe even like me.

Sam is taking us to Rick's engagement party. He's a close friend of theirs, so I presume Jack will be there.

I met Rick once, the last night I saw Mike, before he decided he'd had enough of us. I was sulking at an off comment Mike made about me that I took to heart, and Rick kindly tried to make it better.

"He's like that sometimes, don't worry. You're

special to him," I recall him saying.

I don't know why Rick felt he should console me, since I had just met him, but I've always remembered his kind words. I didn't understand what he meant then, and I still don't, especially considering Mike left me that night.

It's 9:00 p.m., and I'm pacing around the living room, because Sam is a no-show. Marie and I can't go to this party by ourselves, because we don't really know the engaged couple. Plus, her car got a flat tire, today of all days.

"Finally, he's on his way," says Marie. She's walking toward me, just as annoyed as I am at Sam's tardiness. "There's something wrong with his car. It looks like he's going to have to take it to the shop, but he'll be here in ten."

"How's he getting here?"

"Uber," she replies.

೫೫೫

The engagement party is in full force, the music is booming and people are dancing. I thought it'd be a more subdued event.

I spot Jack and Mike as soon as we walk in. They're sitting together at a round table, and there's a girl between them.

Is she with Jack or Mike?

Sam leads us to their table. Mike immediately

gets up and leaves, as expected.

Jack grins, but doesn't get up to kiss me hello. He doesn't do anything he'd normally do, and I assume it's because he's still upset with me.

Then I hear the girl say, "Let's move to another table," to which he replies a resounding, "No."

She's with him!

She's his date!

Shit, what do I do now?

I want to run out the door, but I can't. I'm stuck here, until Sam and Marie decide it's time to leave.

Jack's replaced me, and there is absolutely nothing I can do about it.

I know I deserve it, but damn, it stings!

Marie grabs a few chairs, turns them away from the table, and points at me to sit. I do as she says.

My back is to Jack, but I can feel him...and *her*. She's sulking because Jack said *no* to her. I'm secretly happy he refused her request, and I'm hoping it's because I still have a chance with him.

Sam and Marie are hovering over me. Even Sam knows how awkward this is, and is trying to make me feel at ease. I don't need hovering. I'm going to enjoy myself no matter what. And thanks to Sam's friends, who are approaching me one after the other asking me to dance, I might just have some fun. Why not? If I'm here, I might as well try.

I'm stumped and mortified that Jack actually

brought a date knowing I'd probably be here. I guess it's payback time, and I have to swallow this pill. He's getting even with me. I'm putting up with it because I deserve it, but I'm not giving him the satisfaction of seeing me down, so I smile like the world is my oyster.

Who the hell is that woman!

Mike is back at his old tricks, making sure I know he wants nothing to do with me. As if I care. Every time I get up to dance, he comes back to the table. When I return, he leaves.

Yeah, I get it, Mike. I got it a long time ago...

Jack hasn't moved from the table and neither has his date. I can't look at them. I won't. I just catch glimpses of him when my dance partner spins me in his direction.

He's staring at me...every time!

As soon as I sit down, Sam grabs my hand and squeezes it. Marie smiles at him, grateful to him for protecting me. It's endearing that he's watching out for me, despite my previous inexcusable behavior toward Jack.

This night is turning out to be a bit of a yawn for all three of us. Thankfully, Marie informs me we're leaving, after just a few hours. I need to get home and pick up the pieces of my shattered pride — which I admit this time I helped crush.

Marie's with Sam getting the Uber, but Jack interrupts them. I'm standing a few feet away from them, watching their exchange.

Sam puts his iPhone away, and Jack walks toward me. He's staring at me, as he approaches, his expression unreadable. When he reaches me, he stands right next to me, shoulder to shoulder. My pulse immediately spikes.

What is he doing?

I turn my head and look at him. He gazes back but doesn't smile. He takes my hand and wraps his fingers through mine. "I'll drive you home," he says.

What?

I see a trace of a smile emerging on his lips, his bluish-gray eyes iridescent as they pin me in place.

He's not asking if he can take me home. He's telling me he's doing it, hoping I won't pull away from him.

He doesn't care if *she* sees him holding my hand. It's just him and me again.

I might have a chance to get him back after all.

❧❧❧

What I don't foresee is that *she* is coming with us.

I'm sandwiched between Sam and Marie in the back of Jack's car, and she's in the front with him. I'm feeling all kinds of foolish, and the more I think about how absurd this is, the more confused I become.

It looks like she's had too much to drink and is

going to be sick, because she's bending forward making funny noises.

"Don't you dare barf inside the car. I'll stop if you're feeling sick, but don't make a mess in here," Jack is practically shouting at her.

I've never witnessed intolerant Jack. He's never spoken to me that way...ever. He always treats me with kindness and love.

Selfishly, I don't feel sorry for her. On the contrary, it makes me incredibly happy. Not that he's scolding her, but that I'm sure he would never speak to me in that tone.

I'm about to let out a burst of laughter at the ludicrousness of what's happening, when Marie elbows me lightly on the ribs.

"Owie," I mouth at her, and she shushes me with a knowing smile.

Fifteen minutes later, we're home.

As soon as his car stops in front of our place, I nudge Marie to open the door so I can get out. I say a hasty "goodbye and thank you" to Jack and company, and I'm out like a bullet.

I head straight inside the house. I breathe a sigh of relief that this bizarre evening is over and wait for Marie in the kitchen.

"Well, that was weird," she says cleverly, eyeing me from underneath her lashes.

"I know. He practically yelled at her. Did you see that?" I'm fighting the smile that's refusing to leave my face.

"Everyone saw and heard that, Ellie. Poor girl," she says, though I doubt she really feels sorry for her.

"Yeah..."

"You love it, don't you, because he'd never, ever do that to you?"

"Yeah," I finally smile broadly. "I still hate that he showed up with her. He traded me in pretty quickly," I fret.

"Ellie, if that's a trade in, I feel sorry for her. He stared at you the entire night and drove that poor girl to drink herself under the table," she points out.

I giggle triumphantly, because that's exactly what happened. I'm still important to him despite my inexcusable behavior at our backyard party.

Maybe he'll give me another chance.

꽁꽁꽁

I'm lying on my bed staring at the ceiling with my arms folded behind my head, trying to plan my next step back into Jack's heart.

I need to talk to him. I need to explain myself, and let him know how important he is to me.

Do I call him or text him? Do I ask him to come over or ask him to meet for coffee? A coffee date seems too impersonal. I don't want him to think I don't care after the way I've behaved.

My iPhone pings.
It's 12:00 a.m.
It's Jack — *I smile elated!*

Jack: I had to take her home
Ellie: Ok
Jack: You didn't say goodbye
Ellie: I did you didn't hear me
Jack: I was getting out of the car you didn't wait
Ellie: I didn't think I should you were with her
Jack: I'm sorry
Ellie: For what?
Jack: For not getting out of the car fast enough to grab you
Ellie: I hate that you were with her. I wouldn't have let you touch me
Jack: Don't say that
Ellie: You seemed happy
Jack: Because you were there
Ellie: I should've known you have someone
Jack: I don't
Ellie: It hurts but ok
Jack: Ok what?
Ellie: You have someone you care for
Jack: It's not her
Ellie: Not what it looked like tonight
Jack: Ellie!
Ellie: Jack!
Jack: Don't hate me
Ellie: I can never hate you...
Ellie: But seeing you with her...
Jack: What?
Ellie: You're going to make me say it?
Jack: Yes
Ellie: Kills me
Jack: I'll bring you back to life

Ellie: You always do. I miss you!

Jack: I miss you too

Ellie: So much I can't breathe

Ellie: I'm sorry Jack

Ellie: I wanted to say it on your lips tonight

Ellie: But you were with her!

Jack: Do it tomorrow…today please

Ellie: Yes

Jack: I'll see you later then?

Ellie: Yes

Jack: Go to sleep now Ellie

Ellie: I still hate her

Jack: Ellie!

Ellie: Jack!

Jack: Go to sleep

Ellie: But I want you here with me

Jack: Stop or I'll come over right now

Ellie: Ok!

Jack: Stop Ellie. I'm in bed already

Ellie: Whatcha wearing? 😎😼

Jack: Ellie!

Ellie: Just want to know so I can dream with you

Jack: Dream what?

Ellie: I have a very active imagination

Jack: I'm sure you do

Ellie: I can't wait to see you tomorrow…today

Jack: Me too. I'll be there at 9pm

Ellie: Ok! Good night Jack 😊

Jack: Night Ellie. My Ellie!

Ellie: Yes always! 😊🖤

My Jack, mine, mine, mine!

CHAPTER 21

Time is taking forever. I've been checking my iPhone every five minutes, waiting for 9:00 p.m. to see Jack.

Damn...time is at a standstill.

Tick tock, tick tock...One hour seems to be taking three. Crap!

"Ellie stop, you're driving me crazy! Nine will get here soon enough." Marie is annoyed, because I keep going into her room asking what she's doing.

Since she's not paying attention to me, I've turned into the energizer bunny, running around the house. I've cleaned the kitchen, the bathroom, the living room, my bedroom, and now I'm vacuuming hers.

She's sitting on her bed doing her nails, and she's had enough of me. She grabs me by my arm and pulls me to her. I land on my butt on her bed, startled.

"Stop, Ellie," she laughs. "You've cleaned the entire house, and you hate chores, so stop already. This house is sparkling clean, and you're scaring me."

I'm sweaty and exhausted. I must have burned a thousand calories by now, and it's only 4:00 p.m.

Ugh, time can be so annoying!

"Go take a shower, because you seriously need one," she crinkles her nose, letting me know I stink from all the sweat. "It'll calm you down. Then we'll watch a few movies. That should help distract you and make the time pass faster."

I smell my T-shirt.

Wow, I do stink.

"Okay, just let me finish vacuuming your room, and then I'll stop," I smile and get up.

She shakes her head, amused at how excited I am to see Jack.

☙☙☙

Finally, it's 8:30!

Jack: I'll be there in 20
Ellie: Ok
Jack: Sam's with me

Ellie: Huh?
Jack: He was with me and wanted to come with
Ellie: Huh?
Jack: You're pissed?
Ellie: Huh?
Jack: LOL! You want me to get rid of him?
Ellie: 😊😊 No. I'll tell Marie
Jack: Sam texted her
Ellie: 😵

"I know, Ellie!" Marie shouts from her room.
Of course she does.

It's fine that they're coming along. Marie and Sam's presence will help break any ice that may still linger between Jack and me. Though by the tone of our latest texts, we'll probably be okay, but it never hurts to have a backup plan.

ॐॐॐ

I threw my arms around Jack when I saw him, and he didn't reject me. I kissed him, and he responded to me. His lips remembered mine, and they felt like home. And when those bluish-grays looked at me, the hurt was gone, and all I saw was unbridled warmth.

I can't get enough of him!

We're driving up Pacific Coast Highway, heading to Sycamore Canyon campgrounds. What a random place to take me. His sense of adventure is as unique as he is.

The drive along the coast is beautiful. The ocean is a dark momentous monster to our left, and the headlights of the cars coming and going light the winding road. I'm sure we're the only ones heading to the campgrounds this late at night.

It's tenebrous, dark, and chilly. Even inside the car, I can hear the wind howling and feel the chill of the outside air.

We're creeping slowly through the grounds. The only lights are from the car's headlights. It's almost scary, but I trust Jack, more than I've ever trusted any guy. I always feel safe with him.

Sam is in the back seat talking about ghosts, in attempt to get Marie to lean in closer. It's working, because she's wrapped around him like a vine. I'd be doing the same with Jack, if it was not for the center console between us.

Jack finds a quiet place to park, though in these massive grounds every spot is quiet.

"Hear that? Those are ghosts howling," says Sam in an ominous tone.

"It's not funny, Sam. Stop!" exclaims Marie and slaps his arm, so he'll shut up.

Now Marie and I are terrified of any little noise we hear, and the boys are enjoying every minute of our discomfort.

"Come, let's go watch the stars," Sam opens his door and practically drags a terrified Marie out of the car. She follows him, holding on to his arm for dear life.

Jack and I are finally alone.

He turns on the music on his iPhone. The beautiful sound of John Legend's "All of Me" fills the car.

The perfect song!

"Jack, I'm sorry..." I begin to say my apologies, but he interrupts me.

"No. We're together now, let's concentrate on that," he smiles.

I contemplate him for a few seconds. I know he doesn't want to hear it, but I have to tell him. He has to know what a big mistake it was to pull away from him, how much I've fallen for him.

"Jack, I..." I start, but he stops me with a kiss.

"But..." I try again, and he plants another smooch.

"Please..." I giggle, but he does it again.

I'm not getting anywhere, though I'm perfectly happy if he continues kissing me like this.

I try one more time.

"Jack..." I put a finger on his lips, as he's closing in to kiss me. He quickly removes it and kisses me anyway.

I laugh and he smiles.

I cover his mouth with my hand, but it only encourages him to kiss my palm.

"Okay," I comply, because I sense he doesn't want any reminders of that night.

He removes my hand from his mouth, kisses my fingers, and grins mischievously.

He's up to something.

"Move your seat back all the way, and recline the back rest as far as it'll go," he instructs.

I do as he asks. He steps out of the car and comes around to my side.

"Scoot over," he says slyly, after opening my door.

I do, and he climbs in with me.

We're squeezed together in the passenger seat, facing each other, our legs entangled like pretzels.

"You like John Legend?" I ask, in an attempt to deflect the nervous energy I'm feeling at his close proximity.

He's examining me with his entrancing eyes that sometimes look blue and other times gray. His gaze sends shivers down my body, and I'm aching to touch him again. I can't wait to have his hands on me, to feel my skin tingle at his touch, to see his reaction to mine.

"I enjoy all sorts of music. You'll see," he says but doesn't touch me.

Please touch me, Jack, please!

The Eagles' "Hotel California" fills the car.

He finally lifts his hand to my face, and his fingers caress my cheek, then trace my lips. His eyes look dark gray in the blackness of the night against his black T-shirt.

He kisses me gently on the lips.

"You're so beautiful, Ellie," he whispers softly and pulls at my lower lip with his. "I can stay here forever, tasting your pillowy lips," he whispers against my mouth and deepens the kiss.

My heart swells, and I respond to his thirst.

I briefly pull back to examine him, to see his gorgeous face, to stare at his mesmerizing eyes. He lovingly stares back, removing a strand of hair away from my eyes with his fingers, and kisses me softly again.

As long as he's forgiven me, I can forgive myself. I can love him, really open up my heart to him, and finally allow him love me.

"Ahh, stop, I hate you, Sam!" screams Marie outside, breaking our spell. We both laugh at the echoes of her squealing.

But my hands have a mind of their own, and I slide one under his T-shirt. I skim it across his abs, then move it toward his back and down the inside of his jeans, until I reach the upper half of his behind — it's a tight fit, but I manage.

He gives me a lascivious grin, his eyes burning into mine, and he kisses me deeply, nipping and tugging at my lips with frantic yearning, his tongue caressing mine. He glides his hand underneath my blouse and finds my breast. He pulls down the bra cup and begins to stroke my nipple.

"Mmm," I moan at his expert touch. I dig my

fingers into his behind, pulling him closer to me.

I want him now!

His hand leaves my breast and slides down my stomach, and I know exactly where it's heading.

CHAPTER 22

"Do you want this, Ellie?" Jack whispers on my lips. His hand is already inside my leggings, approaching his goal.

"I can't," I reply shyly between kisses, and he stops.

His lips stop kissing me, his hand halts in place.

I put my hand on his and kiss him lightly. "Let me show you."

I guide his hand down to his goal, and let him explore just long enough for him to feel something blocking his way.

"Shit, you're on your period," he's relieved there's a legitimate reason to my denial.

"Yes, I'm sorry," I say, feeling awkward.

"Not your fault."

Jack may very well be the sexiest man alive, but period sex in the cramped front seat of a car is just not the best choice.

Good thing he has other ideas.

He grabs my hand away from his behind and places it squarely on his bulging crotch. I can feel how ready he is for me.

I'm anxious to feel exactly what I'll be missing thanks to my monthly visitor. I try to unbutton his jeans, but it's proving difficult. Between our two blundering hands, we pop open the button of his jeans. I pull down the zipper and put my hand inside his boxers, while his hand finds its way back to my breast.

He's hard, big, thick...

I gaze into his eyes, kiss him, and tug at his lip with mine. My hand is working him up and down, squeezing and stroking over and over.

"Mmm, this is what I'm missing," I whisper on his lips.

"Mmm, baby," he grumbles between groans.

His mouth is on mine, kissing me deeply, imploring, begging me not to stop pleasuring him. I squeeze and stroke him again, while his lips and tongue play with mine. I savor his moans in my mouth.

I imagine him inside me, and my heart rate picks up along with his. His fingers are stroking and tugging at my nipple, and the tension gets deeper as he's closer to his release. He's close, really close, and I'm desperate to bring him to pure bliss. I stroke him faster and harder.

I suck on his lower lip with mine, and he explodes in my hand.

"Fuck, baby!"

He opens his eyes and watches me sated, pleased, and gratified, before he kisses me softly again. He's breathing hard, and I'm grinning from ear to ear thrilled by my accomplishment.

My hand is still inside his boxers holding him, and it's wet, very wet.

He opens the glove compartment, grabs a few napkins, pulls my hand out of his boxers, and cleans it. There's a bit of him left on my ring finger, so I put it in my mouth and suck it clean.

He gapes at me surprised, before kissing me softly and murmuring, "My Ellie."

"Yes," I reply, "My Jack."

Adele's "One and Only" is playing, tainting me with yearning for him.

"Let me be your one and only, Jack," I say softly, as Adele sings everything I want to say to him.

He closes his eyes briefly, taking in the lyrics.

"You have no idea what you mean to me, Ellie," he whispers.

"I do have an idea, Jack, because you mean that much to me too." I trace his face with my fingers and kiss him along the way...the beautiful arch of his nose, his eyelids, his forehead, his lips...

I want to kiss his lips forever!

"Mmm," he sighs, each time my lips touch him.

He smiles, making my heart leap.

Seeing him, having him next to me, and knowing he's given me another chance is my lifeline. I don't fear loving him anymore.

My past is gone and buried, where it belongs. Jack is my present. I pray he knows how much I love him, and that I will never let him down again.

༒ ༒ ༒

I'm having a hard time staying awake at my desk. Were it not for the immense amount of work I have to finish today, and my elated state thanks to last night's adventure with Jack at the campgrounds, I would pass out this second. Not to mention it's Monday.

But it's almost 3:00 p.m., and I just have one more hour, before I can head home to get some sleep.

My iPhone pings.

Marie: Ellie I have something to tell you
Ellie: Spill it
Marie: Promise you won't be mad
Ellie: Promise it won't make me mad
Marie: Just promise
Ellie: Ok Marie just tell me cause you're making me nervous

Marie: Mike called needs a favor
Ellie: So?
Marie: He wants you to help too
Ellie: Huh?
Marie: He needs volunteers
Ellie: Ugh why me? We'll talk when I get home ok
Marie: Yep

જાજાજા

As soon as I get home, I head straight to bed. I need to sleep just enough to be able to face this nonsense about Mike.

I don't know how he could have the nerve to request my help after the way he's treated me. Every time I've seen him he runs away from me like I'm a leper.

But now that *he* needs something...

I'm snuggling under the sheets fast asleep, when I feel a hand stirring me.

"Ellie, wake up." Marie is sitting on the bed.

"Let's talk later," I try to get her to go away and let me be.

"It is later. It's 8:00. I thought I'd wake you so you can get things ready for tomorrow. Otherwise, you're going to be late to work in the morning."

I feel drowsy, in need of more sleep. I could've sworn I fell asleep just fifteen minutes ago. I reluctantly prop myself up and recline my head on the headboard. I rub my eyes, so maybe they'll stay open.

"Now that you're up," she teases. I roll my eyes at her, but she continues, "what should I tell Mike?"

"About what?" I say drowsily.

"About you helping."

"I don't know, Marie. The last thing I want is to get involved with Mike again. It's awkward and unnecessary."

Why is he okay with me all of a sudden? I've put up with too much from him already. He's way past his allotted rudeness.

"Sam and Jack are helping..." she prompts, but I hold my hand up to her so she stops talking for a second.

I grab my iPhone and check for texts from Jack. Sure enough, I have several, the last one an hour ago.

I continue ignoring Marie and text him.

> **Ellie: Sorry baby I fell asleep Marie just woke me**
> **Jack: Long fun night last night?**
> **Ellie: Maybe**
> **Jack: Who with?**
> **Ellie: A handsome sexy guy**
> **Jack: Mmm did he treat you right?**
> **Ellie: He did but he could've done better**
> **Jack: Do explain**
> **Ellie: He offered but the circumstances didn't permit though I think I did a good job**
> **Jack: Did you now... Any proof?**
> **Ellie: I licked it!** 🍪🍫
> **Jack: Yes you did baby and I promise to return the favor!**

Ellie: Yes please

I'm grinning like a goof, as I read his texts.

Marie takes me by my shoulders and shakes me forcefully to pay attention to her.

"I can see Jack's got you wrapped around his finger, *or something else*, but we need to finish the discussion."

I playfully stick my tongue out at her and broaden the in-love grin that's already on my face.

I continue texting Jack.

Ellie: Hold that thought baby Marie needs to talk to me BRB 😵
Jack: Ok baby xo

I put the cell down and look up at Marie.

"First, tell me what this whole thing is about. What is Mike doing that he needs to recruit so many people?"

Apparently, the firm where Mike is interning or working, Marie isn't quite sure, is doing a voter registration event. With the upcoming elections, they have partnered with a local, non-partisan organization.

So far so good...

They're setting up stations all over Los Angeles to register people to vote. One of Mike's tasks is to recruit as many volunteers as possible, because each station needs three to four people, and that's a "whole lot of peeps," Marie mocks.

"If I do it, and that's a big *if*, what would be required?" I ask, hoping I can find an excuse to say no.

"We'll all attend a meeting this Saturday at the Four Seasons, where we'll get the rundown of what we're expected to do, how to approach people, what information they'll need to fill out, etc. And the actual event is the following Saturday," she explains.

I stare at her for a minute, contemplating if I should do this. I don't want Jack to think I'm doing it because I want anything to do with Mike, but on the other hand, it is important to register as many voters as possible.

Mike's cause seems to be legit...

"I need to check with Jack first."

"As you should," she agrees.

"Just so there won't be any misunderstandings."

"Yep, I get it. Let me know," she smiles.

I dread bringing this up to Jack. We just had a kinky text exchange, and I don't want to bring down his mood...or mine, for that matter.

But Marie is badgering me for an answer. I gather from her tone that Mike's been pestering her.

It's better to tell Jack sooner rather than later.

Ellie: Hey baby still awake?
Jack: Yes thinking dirty thoughts about you

Ellie: You'll have to show me in person
Jack: Count on it!
Ellie: I'm going to need a cold shower! 😅🐱
Ellie: I want to share something with you
Jack: Shoot
Ellie: Marie just told me about a volunteer thing of
    Mike's. Wants me to help wanted to run it by you

I wait for his answer...

Come on, Jack, this means nothing. Please don't be upset...

Jack: It's fine. I'm going to help, I'll protect you
Ellie: I don't need protection. I need you!
Jack: You have me
Ellie: 😊💕 You sure it's ok? I'm not really interested
Jack: Yes it's a good cause
Ellie: Ok I miss you
Jack: I miss you too
Ellie: Talk later going to take that shower 😅
Jack: Think of me
Ellie: Mmm cold shower it is! 🐱😊
Jack: LOL night baby
Ellie: Night xoxo

CHAPTER 23

It's Saturday morning, and Marie is nudging me to get up — *I'm so not a morning person.*

We have to be at the Four Seasons for the voter registration training by 9:00 a.m. Apparently, it's going to be at least four hours long.

Why did I agree to do this?

The only consolation, and frankly motivation, is that Jack will be there. We've both been so busy that I haven't seen him since Sunday.

How is it we manage to have such kinky text exchanges but can't find time in the evenings to see each other?

᧞᧞᧞

The training is in a large conference room. There are rectangular tables set up in two rows, each seating eight people.

When we arrive, Jack, Sam, Mike, and Mario are already seated with other people. They smile and wave hello but don't get up to greet us. I figure it's because we're very late, and the training is about to start.

Marie and I find two available spots located a couple of rows behind theirs. Jack is sitting directly in front of me, and I'm hoping he'll turn around and blow me a kiss.

He doesn't.

Since it would be rude of me to distract him with texts, I refrain, but I'm aching to kiss him.

We're given specific instructions on everything from how to approach people, to what information they need to fill out and what to do with the registration cards. It's actually very interesting, because I enjoy politics.

Four and a half hours later the training is over, and Marie and I join the guys. We greet them as usual with a kiss on the cheek. Even Mike emulates the gesture, and thanks us for helping. The thank you is even directed at *me*, and he actually looks me in the eyes.

Well, that's a shocker!

Jack is watching me closely, and I can see he's tense. Is he looking for evidence I'm still hung up on Mike? He won't find any. I'm cordial with him, though he doesn't deserve it, but I'm not showing him any special treatment. I'm over that hang up.

"Do you need a ride home?" asks Jack.

I think he's trying to find a way to be with me, without drawing suspicion.

Why is he hiding our relationship? Weren't we passed that?

He has to be aware of the rejection I feel by pretending our relationship is still in the friend-zone. Unless...Is that what I am to him, just a friend with benefits?

The thought seriously disturbs me.

"Marie drove," I answer him pensive, in a sedated tone.

He looks down, discouraged. He knows I'm vexed but doesn't know how to fix it.

It's an easy fix. Take me in your arms and kiss me, tadah!

"Enjoy the rest of your day," Mike says to us, before slipping his arm around Jack's shoulders, "We're having a boys' night."

It's an insinuation, though I don't think it's meant to stir up trouble between Jack and me. I doubt he has any idea of what's going on with us.

"Well, enjoy. See ya," snaps Marie and nods at me to follow her.

I give them a barely there smile and walk away.

❧❧❧

"I know you better than you know yourself. You're upset, right?" Marie begins her interrogation on the drive home.

"Why did Jack act like that? It's like he's ashamed of me. He could've sat with me. He could've put his arm around me, shown me *some* affection," I respond, not quite understanding why he was so indifferent.

"They're best friends, Ellie. I'm not justifying Jack's actions, but it's going to take time before he can truly feel comfortable showing you open affection in front of Mike. Dating your best friend's ex is kind of taboo, even if it was Mike who left you. There's a code between guy friends that states they can't date each other's exes. A code Jack has broken. I don't think it's an easy thing for him to admit to Mike. And, not to bring up the past, but when Jack was ready to put it all on the line for you, you pulled away from him." She eyes me nervously, hoping she didn't just stab me in the heart with her candid observation.

"I. Don't. Care!" I stomp my feet forcefully and pout petulantly.

Marie peers at me from underneath her lashes, her eyes narrowed, and she's grinning.

I burst out laughing.

"I knew it!" she laughs, confirming my moody

reaction was a joke.

We're both laughing so hard we have to make a pee stop at the nearest gas station — not the first time that's happened since we've known each other.

᪥᪥᪥

"Since the boys are going out who knows where, what do you want to do this beautiful Saturday night?" Marie asks.

It's late in the evening, and I haven't heard from Jack. I'm letting it be and not reaching out to him. I don't want to be clingy — which I've actually never been — and I won't start now.

Let him have his boys' night out. I'll have a girls' night out and thoroughly enjoy it.

"Let's go out dancing and enjoy this wonderful weather. Let's dance, baby, dance!" I throw my hands up in the air and twirl around.

"Yes, yes, yes!" Marie is practically jumping up and down exhilarated at my excitement.

"Definitely an Uber night!" she says thrilled.

"Definitely!" I wink at her.

᪥᪥᪥

Marie called it when she picked the Rooftop at The Standard hotel. It's packed with beautiful people, and my mind is solely focused on having a good time.

Neither Jack nor anyone else will ruin this night.

We're surrounded by gorgeous, available men, and I feel free. Free of stress. Free of worry. Free of expectations. Free, just a 23-year-old spending one helluva night with her best friend.

Marie's been taking pictures and posting them on Instagram. I swear her entire life is superbly documented on IG.

"Selfie!" she yells and pulls me in. She snaps a picture of us puckering up in the air.

Yea, we look adorable!

She uploads it and captions it, **Offering Free Kisses!** 💋🤍💋💋 **#girlsnightout #hottiesindahouse**

The next one is a shot of me dancing, holding a mojito in one hand and the other hand up in the air. **That's My Girl!** 💚🍸😍 **#shesacatch #bff**

She follows it with another one of us posing, showing off our very short dresses, and very high heels that make our legs look long and sultry. **Mojitos Baby!!!** 🎶🍸🍸🎶 **#girlshavingfun**

The next one is a group shot of us with five hot guys, none of which we actually know. Marie asked them to get in the picture with us, and they were more than happy to oblige. **Blessed Among Men!** 💋💋💋 **#kisses #surroundedbyhotties #bff**

The picture that has the most consequences is one she takes next. After the group photo with the hotties, one of them makes a funny remark, which after three mojitos, I find hilarious. I'm laughing so hard, I almost fall backward, and he puts his hand slightly on my waist to hold me up. She captions it, *When A Guy Makes You Laugh... Checkmate!* 💋 💧😊 *#goelliegoellie #loveher*

CHAPTER 24

My iPhone is blowing up inside my boob. It's buzzing nonstop, and I'm getting quite the sensual massage. I excuse myself and head to the restroom to see who's so desperate to reach me.

I dig inside my boob to pull out the iPhone. A girl washing her hands at the sink gives me a knowing look. Yea, she knows boobs are the perfect substitute for pockets, when we don't want to carry a purse. They're multipurpose.

I see at least five texts in a row from Jack.

My eyesight is blurry, surely from all drinks I've had. I giggle hysterically and walk out of the restroom to show Marie.

When I find her, she has two fresh mojitos in her hands. I trade her one for my iPhone. She smirks at the texts and hands the device back to me.

"Did you tag the pictures with our location?" I ask between sips of my drink.

She shakes her head no.

"Good."

I'm having too much fun to have Jack or Sam suddenly show up to ruin things. He chose to go out with Mike. I choose to have a great night with my best friend.

I'm doing nothing wrong.

The iPhone rings. Jack's name pops on the screen. I immediately hand it to Marie.

She gapes at me, "You don't want to answer?"

I shake my head no.

"You want *me* to answer?"

I anxiously nod yes.

"Heeello, yep, Marie. No, she's in the restroom right now. Yep, we're good. Yep, I'm sure. Okay, okay, I will. Bye." She hangs up and hands me the cell.

I'm glaring at her waiting to hear what Jack said.

"Fine," she giggles. "He wanted to talk to you and make sure you're safe. He said to call him."

"Okay," I slur, "Salud!"

He shouldn't be upset, and I'm in too good a mood to pause for a contentious call with him. He'll have to wait until tomorrow.

The cell pings again with more texts, from Jack I presume. I look at it, but the battery is on red. It's about to die, and unfortunately, I don't have a charger in my boob. I'll call him tomorrow.

స్రోస్రోస్రో

I walk into the kitchen at a quarter past noon and find Marie still in her PJs. She looks like she just woke up too, but at least she's functional. She's making two bloody marys. She knows I hate them, but it's the only thing that's going help with this nasty hangover. My head is pounding.

"Sam's asking about you," she leans against the counter and raises her iPhone to show me.

"Why?"

"Hmm, because Jack can't get a hold of you," she chuckles.

"Oh, that. The phone's battery died, and in the state we got home last night, I totally forgot to charge it. I'll reach out to him when I've showered, and my brain is back online," I sit at the table to drink the bloody cocktail she's prepared for me.

She can't believe I'm not running out of the room to check Jack's texts and explain myself to him. Last night I had genuine fun, and I met some very nice guys. I'm not interested in any of them of course, because frankly Jack is the only guy that takes my breath away.

But this new me is taking control of her life and being responsible for her own decisions. I am the only one that can make me happy, not Jack or any other man. It's a cop-out to place the burden of my happiness, or lack thereof, on someone else.

I admit it's taken me a while to come to this realization, but I'm here, and I'm not going back. I love Jack, and I want to be with him, but he has to want to be with me too.

"I'm proud of you," says Marie, as if she knows what I'm thinking. She kisses me lightly on the top of my head and walks out of the kitchen.

"I'm taking a shower," she blurts out, "finish that drink."

I'm proud of myself too.

Rob was right, how lucky am I to have found Jack. I didn't even have to go looking for him. I really should thank Sam.

But I have to know where I stand with him and what his intentions are. Does he really care for me, or am I just a game he's enjoying between girl-friends? He's never made me feel that way, but his actions are sometimes questionable. There has to be something more than that damn code Marie keeps bringing up.

Jack has been Mike's friend since they were kids, and I'm sure that weighs on him. But he's also made it clear I'm important to him. He proves it to me with every text, every word he says to me, every touch.

So, what is it, Jack?

৵৵৵

I'm showered, my hair is dry, and I'm wearing my most comfy PJs. I feel so much better thanks to the shower and that awful drink Marie made for me.

I'm sitting on my bed with my legs crossed, preparing to deal with Jack. I'm slightly disheart-ened. I won't take his crap, if that's what his texts were about.

He would never...

Just in case, I've made up my mind that I'm going to stand my ground.

I did nothing wrong!

I sigh, turn on my iPhone, and begin to read...

Jack: You're having fun...
Jack: Not that I don't want you to
Jack: You look beautiful
Jack: That's a very short dress
Jack: I've had those stunning legs wrapped around mine
Jack: Another drink or the same one?
Jack: Still drinking?
Jack: Where are you? Tell me I'll go get you
Jack: Answer me!
Jack: Why aren't you answering me?
Jack: I see why
Jack: Who's the guy? He's touching you
Jack: He shouldn't be fucking touching you!

Jack: You look happy. I want to make you that happy

Jack: That smile is mine!

Jack: I wanted to see you

Jack: But you're there with that fucker

Jack: Tell me you're home safe

Jack: Please call me

Jack: Text me or something…

Jack: ANSWER ME Ellie

Jack: Waiting…

Jack: I'll wait all night

Jack: ALL FUCKING NIGHT!

Jack: I'M NOT FUCKING KIDDING!

CHAPTER 25

Jack's waiting to hear from me. It's been hours since I told Marie I'd call him. I don't want to make him wait any longer.

I thought his texts would be reproachful or accusatorial, but they're not. He's worried about me, worried about us, and that I get. I'm worried about us too.

I call him.

"Hi," he says quietly, picking up on the first ring.

"Hi," I reply.

"Are you okay?" he asks softly.

"Yes."

"You had a good night, then?" his tone thoughtful.

"Yes. How was your boys' night?"

"Not as fun," he answers somberly.

"I'm sorry."

"Not your fault. I didn't stay long," he says.

"Hmm, are you okay?"

"No." He sounds so bleak. It hurts to hear it.

"What's wrong?"

"I wanted to be with you last night."

"But you went out with your boys," I remind him.

"You were having a lot of fun."

"I was," I reply honestly.

He sighs.

"But that doesn't mean I didn't miss you," I confess.

"I'm glad you missed me," he replies relieved.

We both remain quiet for a few seconds. I don't know what else to say. Should I bring up that it upset me when he didn't show me any affection after the training?

It seems petty after all this.

"You're working tomorrow?" he finally breaks the silence.

"Yes, why?"

"I'd like to hold you right now," he says.

"You can, if you want to."

"Can I come by?"

"Yes."

"On my way," he replies quickly, and we hang up.

❧❧❧

"Ellie, someone's here to see you," shouts Marie.

I'm in my bedroom, lying on my bed watching a movie, my head resting on a pillow propped against the headboard.

"Hey," Jack opens the door but doesn't walk in. He's hesitant, standing at my bedroom door, not entirely sure how I'm going to receive him.

I open my arms to reassure him.

He grins and walks in. He crawls into bed, kisses me on the lips and snuggles me. He places his head on my chest, wraps his arm around my waist and sighs, as if he's been holding it in for days.

I feel awful seeing him like this. I didn't mean to upset him, but I also saw no harm in going out and having fun, when he was doing the same.

I run my fingers through his hair and gently stroke his ear.

"Mission Impossible III?" he asks.

"Mhm," I reply.

"Nice. Can I stay?"

"Yes," I say softly, because nothing would make me happier.

He gets up and removes his clothes, keeping only his boxers. He looks delectable. I'm aching to feel the warmth of his body next to me. But he also looks drained, his bluish-grays weary.

"You're exhausted, aren't you?" I ask concerned.

"Yes," he confesses. "I didn't sleep waiting to

hear from you. I told you I'd wait up all night."

I sigh and shake my head.

My stubborn Jack.

He's caught between his love for me and his loyalty to his friend. I briefly put myself in his shoes. How would I feel if Marie all of a sudden started dating Mike? Even though I don't love him anymore, I admit I'd hate it. I'd think it's disloyal, insensitive, and cruel.

Maybe there is something to this "code" thing between guy friends. Perhaps Jack and I did break it, but we didn't do it intentionally. Code or not, it's too late for me. I love him.

I lift the sheets so he can get back in bed. He happily snuggles next to me in exactly the same position as before. I stroke his hair gently, and he falls asleep almost immediately.

The movie is over, but it's only 8:00 p.m., and I'm not sleepy. I search the guide for another one and settle on reruns of Games of Thrones.

I nudge Jack gently, and he stirs just enough for me to scurry down so my pillow and head are on the bed. He doesn't let go of me. I kiss him gently on the forehead and get back to the perils of GOT.

A few hours later, I've had enough and turn off the TV. I nudge Jack a bit again, so I can move from under his embrace. I manage it, lie on my side, and watch him sleep.

He looks so peaceful, and his beautiful face is now worry-free. I kiss him lightly on the lips, and gently run the tips of my fingers through his hair. He doesn't wake, but the tiniest smile forms on his lips, and I sigh in love.

I'm longing to make love to him, but I don't have the heart to wake him. It's my fault he's so beat, and he has to work tomorrow. He won't be at the top of his game, if he isn't well rested.

I can't believe he didn't sleep last night, because I went out with Marie. I understand why he felt threatened, after seeing the pictures Marie posted on IG. It was my fault. I egged her on. I wanted him to see me happy without him. But the truth is I want him, only him. I want him in my bed forever — preferably conscious because I have carnal plans for us. But tonight, I get to watch him sleep, and somehow, this feels even more intimate.

I turn off the lights, and lie on my back. He wraps his arm around me again, one of his legs between mine, and he buries his face in the nape of my neck.

"My Ellie," he sighs quietly.

I fall into a blissful sleep, because he's here with me.

≈≈≈

Waking up with Jack felt familiar, intimate, and

natural. I wonder why? He's never been in my bed before. But it's very clear to me that this is how we belong...together.

I'm dressed and ready to head out to work with Marie. I couldn't bring myself to wake him when I got up, and I'm glad, because I got to watch him sleep again.

I sit on the bed next to him and kiss him lightly on the lips. He opens his eyes.

"Morning, baby," I smile at him.

He smiles back content and relaxed. "I love waking up with you," he pulls me in for another soft kiss.

"Me too, baby. Thank you for coming over," I run my fingers through his hair.

"Thank you for inviting me."

"I have to get to work, but stay and rest a bit more. I'll text you later," I contemplate him.

He's so damn gorgeous, and he's naked in my bed!

I bite my lip and move to get up, before I decide to call in sick and make love to him all day long. He pulls me down to him and nibbles at my earlobe.

"Okay, baby," he whispers. "I'll stay just a minute longer, because your scent is on this pillow."

I pull away and give him a dazzling, love struck smile. My heart is fluttering just looking at him. The worry in his eyes is gone. He's happy and content. I'm thrilled I have something to do with it. I lean down and kiss him again.

I can barely make myself leave him, but I do.

He won't stay long after I leave. I'm certain he has to be at his office soon.

Looking back as I exit my room, I imagine what our life together could be like.

It looks pretty damn amazing from here!

Yet we have a serious conversation pending, if we're going to have a real chance at making it. He can't have reservations about my love and commitment to him, and I can't doubt his for me. I'm going to give him some space and not push him to tell Mike about us, not yet. That's going to be one volcanic conversation, when it actually happens. Maybe it should be me that tells Mike. I'll run it by him at some point.

CHAPTER 26

Later today, I have another, and hopefully last, interview at the magazine.

Jack knows how important this is to me and has been very encouraging. He's my number one supporter and always makes me feel like I can do anything.

I arrive to the interview with a clear mind and an open heart. If it's meant to be, the job is mine.

"Hi, Ellie, it's nice to meet you," Angela Richards, the magazine's publisher welcomes me.

"I'm glad to be here, Mrs. Richards," I shake her hand and sit across from her.

The previous interviews were with the head of HR and the VP of editorial, but Mrs. Richards is the one I really have to impress. It's her decision who gets the job. From what I've been told, there are just two of us left in the running.

She's a lovely, tall woman in her mid-fifties, if I had to guess. She's very smart, and I hope I'm as accomplished as she is someday. I feel comfortable meeting her. I get the sense she expects perfection, but she also values autonomy.

As the editor of a section of the magazine, I would be entirely responsible for deciding what is printed in those pages, as well as the online presence.

I like the old school feel of a paper magazine. It's a miracle it's still being printed in this day and age. It speaks volumes of its power in the industry.

"You have a remarkable resume for someone so young. Your internships at Columbia College are very diverse. My staff has been very impressed with you thus far. I just have a few questions."

She asks me about my love and knowledge of music, whether I can handle covering different music genres, and how I feel about interviewing, not only artists, but executives. She's impressed by my portfolio, approving the mix of serious and light tones in my writing. She also mentions they are planning on launching an online presence in Spanish and praises my bilingual skills.

"I've really enjoyed meeting you, Ellie. We will make a decision very soon," Mrs. Richards says with a sincere smile. "One last question, you have the option of making Los Angeles your base, or you can choose New York. We would prefer Los Angeles, of course, but we also feel that a happy editor is a great editor. We will support your decision to move, if that's your choice. If hired, would you stay in Los Angeles?"

"Yes, I have no reason to move at this moment," I reply honestly.

"Great. Thank you for coming, Ellie. We'll be in touch soon," she stands, and we say goodbye.

I leave the interview feeling confident that I did a great job. I answered all the questions with professionalism and assertiveness. This position is a perfect fit for me. I hope they choose me.

Now, I wait.

❧❧❧

Tomorrow is the voter registration event, but right now I'm excited about seeing Jack. He called and said he'd be here as soon as he could, which could mean an hour or so. He sounded a bit tired. I almost told him not to come over, but I miss him.

The doorbell rings, and Marie runs to open the front door.

Maybe she's expecting someone.

"Hey, Ellie, Mike's here." She's standing at my bedroom door. "He's just checking that we're set for tomorrow morning. I told him I'll be leaving early."

"Because of the concert you're going to?"

"Yep. Eh, he wants to talk to you," she says with hesitation.

"Me? Why?"

"He said he just wants to make sure that you'll be there."

"What? I'm getting ready. Jack will be here soon. Tell him I'm in," I reply distracted.

"I did. He insisted."

"Seriously, Marie?"

She gives me an I-don't-know-how-to-get-rid-of-him shrug.

I sigh bothered.

I'm in an old pair of shorts, a huge Columbia College Chicago sweatshirt, and a pair of old flip-flops, because I don't care what he thinks of me.

I head outside, where he's leaning against his dark blue Mazda A3. Marie's with me for moral support.

"Hey, Mike, what's up?" I smile at him, but my arms are crossed. That should give him a clue about the resentment I harbor for being forced out here to talk to him.

He fails to notice.

"Hi," he replies unfazed.

This is the second greeting he's given me since he left me.

What's up with that?

I silently wait for him to answer my original question.

"Just, you know, want to confirm you are set for tomorrow. Marie tells me she'll be leaving early. Will you be there the entire time?" he asks.

"Yea," I reply. "I've got nowhere else to be."

"Oh, okay, sounds good. Well, thanks for helping. I really appreciate it," he's still grinning, as if I'm supposed to be impressed.

"Of course, no problem," I offer him a weak smile.

"Well, I'll let you guys get back to your Friday night plans. I might have some of my own," he replies smirking.

Ugh, that same smirk I would've fallen over some time ago, that same smirk I now find appalling.

"Okay, nice to see you, Mike. Bye," I say with the friendliest tone I can muster and walk back in the house.

Marie follows me into the living room.

"That's why he wanted to see me? He wants me to know he has plans tonight. Ugh!" I say to Marie with a cross tone. I roll my eyes and head back to my room to get dressed. She shrugs, like she's just as bewildered as I am by Mike's behavior.

Twenty minutes later, Jack arrives, and Sam is right behind him. I'm glad he's here earlier than expected but grateful he didn't bump into Mike.

"He stopped by as I was leaving my apartment," Jack says in my ear when he embraces me, referring to Sam.

I don't mind.

Despite the fact he looks freshly showered, he can't hide how tired he is. I feel safer knowing Sam is around in case he's too worn-out to drive back. And knowing Jack's spontaneity, we'll probably head to San Diego to watch the sunrise.

ও ও ও

"Let's just drive away from LA," suggests Jack.

It's almost midnight by the time we get on the road. We spent hours at home listening to music, before deciding to go out.

We're heading toward Pasadena.

The quaint town appears deserted. The only thing open is probably an IHOP.

Jack seems a bit irritated — *he must have had a rough day.*

"Are you okay, baby?" I take his hand.

"Yes, as long as I'm with you. This place is desolate though, everything looks closed," his tone subdued.

We're parked on a side street consulting our apps hoping to find somewhere to go. We're not familiar with Pasadena, and we're not finding anything appealing to do.

"That's okay, we can go home. You look really tired," I lean over the middle console of the car to kiss him.

He kisses me back and starts the car.

I absentmindedly ask, "Isn't Mount Baldy around here?"

"Yep, over that way," he points outside his window.

I don't think about it again. I'm distracted by Marie and Sam, who are playfully arguing about the best frozen yogurt flavors, of all things. Their fights are very funny.

I'm not sure if they're dating or just friends with benefits. Whatever it is, she certainly enjoys his company, but I don't sense she wants anything serious with him. I'll have to ask her about it later.

I turn to Jack, and I notice we're not heading home.

"Isn't the way to Culver City that way?" I point in the opposite direction of where we're heading.

"Yea," he responds.

"Where are we going?"

"Mount Baldy," he grins.

I smile overjoyed. He's doing this for me.

Mount Baldy is not just *over there*, it's at least an hour and a half away.

Only my Jack!

CHAPTER 27

I suspect it's around 2:00 a.m. when we're just beginning to make our way up Baldy. It's dark and creepy — creepier than the camping grounds.

The higher we get, the colder it feels. The road is sparkling. Although there isn't any snow this time of year, it's cold enough that it's glistening with what looks like hoarfrost.

It's so beautiful!

I should find this venture unnerving, but I don't even think about the possibility of any danger. I'm going on an adventure with Jack, and he'll protect me.

That's the only thing that matters.

Besides, he's driving slowly and carefully. He will make sure we get to the top safely.

What *is* scary are the horror stories that Sam is recounting...again. This time it's beheaded zombies that dwell in the mountain.

"See that light over there," he points to what looks like a fire burning in the distance. "That's where the witch that inhabits this mountain lives. She controls the zombies that are buried all along this mountain. They come out at night to hunt and kill those that disturb their peace. There's one right there!" he shouts.

Marie squeals in horror.

I'm laughing, pretending his scare tactics aren't getting to me. Jack kisses my hand from time to time to keep me calm and chuckles at Sam's childish tales.

We make it to the top safely. I have no sense of time, nor do I know how long it's taken us to get here. Jack finds a place to park away from any prying eyes — not that there are any this time of night. I'm sure we're the only crazy ones up here this late.

We get out of the car to take in the panoramic view.

It's stunning!

It's really cold and windy. Jack puts his arms around me to protect me from the biting chill. He's got a jacket on, but I don't. I should've worn jeans instead of this short skirt, but I would've never guessed we'd end up at the peak of Baldy. At least

I'm wearing a long sleeve blouse and closed toe booties. But on this wintry mountain, I might as well be wearing a bikini.

We're taking in the world before us through a whole new lens.

Wow, the vastness!

Rows and rows of gigantic trees now sit below us, the dark sky their blanket and the stars their nightlight.

I feel on top of the world.

"Let's go explore," Jack tugs at my hand.

The rational part of my brain switches on, and I resist his invitation.

"It's too dark and dangerous to go exploring," I say sweetly. I pull him into an embrace, slide my arms inside his jacket, and rest my head on his chest.

I'm shivering.

He holds me tightly and kisses my forehead.

"You're right," he admits.

Marie and Sam get back in the car. They'd rather be warm inside, than freeze out here, even if the view is breathtaking. I imagine they also want to give us some privacy.

Jack walks me to the back of the car, opens the trunk, and grabs a large, very soft, light blue throw.

Why would he have a throw?

"My sister," he says, as if he just heard my thoughts. "Sometimes she borrows my car."

I smile relieved and head with him to the front of the car. He helps me up on the hood, throws the soft material around my shoulders, and pulls me into him.

He's standing between my legs, his hands on my hips. I take the edges of the throw, wrap it around him too, and hold it close with one hand. We're cocooned in an embrace.

I'm secretly thanking his sister for borrowing his car and providing this warm blanket.

We stay like this for what seems like hours, kissing and admiring the beautiful view. We're in the clouds, floating above everyone and everything, in our own little piece of heaven. One that I'm lucky enough to enjoy thanks to this spontaneous, adorable, loving guy I've fallen in love with.

It's so peaceful up here.

The only sound is the wind singing with the trees and our breathing.

"How do you do it?" I look at him adoringly.

"Do what, baby?" he asks bemused.

"Make me so happy," I stroke the back of his neck with my fingers.

"Do I make you happy?"

"Of course you do," I say candidly.

I hope he can see it.

"I'm glad I make you happy. I want to experience new things with you, Ellie. Create unique memories that are just ours. You inspire me."

"And so you brought me to the top of a mountain?" I giggle. "Only you, Jack Milian."

"Is that a good or not so good only me?" He frowns.

"It's a fantastic only you. It's a perfect only you. I'm in awe of you, Jack. I'm in awe of how you make me feel, of what I feel for you," I say sweetly and kiss him softly.

He gazes at me uncertain, like he has no idea I've fallen irrevocably in love with him.

"You're right here, Jack," I take his hand and place it on my heart, holding it tightly against my chest.

He sighs. "You're in here too," he takes my hand, kissed it, and then places it against his heart.

I fall for him even harder...

"Please never doubt how important you are to me," I plead.

"You may have to remind me once in a while," he says with an uneasy grin.

"Why? You don't believe me?"

"I just like hearing you say it," he says.

But his tentative eyes tell me there's more to it, another reason he's not sharing with me. I thought we had put the incident at Marie's party behind us. That he had forgiven me for pulling away from him. If that's not the reason for his trust issues, then what is it?

"I will remind you. Only because I like the sound

of it leaving my lips," I kiss him softly, "which belong entirely to you."

He stares at me, searching my eyes for the
truth. I hope he can see how absolutely sure I am
of my love for him. How he's turned my world
right side up. That he owns my heart.

Please believe me, Jack, please.

He doesn't respond. He just kisses me softly on
the lips over and over and crushes me to him. I
hope it means he believes me.

We look like the cutest couple tenderly
embracing. What only he and I know is that his
hand has made its way up my skirt, between my
thighs. His expert fingers have moved my panties
out of his way, and he's there, exploring. His other
hand is on my back holding me tightly in place.

I've unzipped him too, and one hand is on his
erection, the other still around his neck, holding
the throw securely around us.

We're loving each other with our hands and lips,
in the quiet of the mountain, under the privacy the
throw is affording us.

He's intent on pleasuring me, on returning the
favor, like he promised.

He moves slightly to one side of me, so he can
get a better grip. I'm forced to release him. I take
my hand from inside his jeans and place it on his
shoulder.

Sam and Marie have a clear line of sight to us,

but I dismiss my embarrassment at the thought that they might know what's happening inside our bubble.

He slides two fingers inside me and starts thrusting, pushing and circling them hard, fast then slowly, putting pressure on my most sensitive spot again and again.

"Mmm," I moan quietly, my forehead resting on his shoulder. I'm trying hard to muffle my moans, but the feeling is intense.

I lift my head and kiss his earlobe, nibble it and bite it.

"Ahh, baby," he reacts quietly to my assault but doesn't halt his fingers.

I kiss his cheek, then the side of his mouth, then take his lower lip with my tongue and lips. He responds by kissing me as deeply and passionately, as his fingers are working me. His mouth is absorbing my moans, as his fingers are thrusting inside of me.

"Feel it, baby," he whispers between kisses. "You're mine, Ellie. Come for me, baby."

A few more thrusts and I explode gloriously on his fingers.

"Yours," I sigh on his lips satisfied and open my eyes to look at him.

He's grinning, proud of himself, and kisses me gently again.

He takes his fingers out of me, brings them to

his mouth, and sucks.

"Mmm," he praises, "my sweet, mouthwatering Ellie."

I stare at him, grinning. He has indeed returned the favor, splendidly.

Sam approaches slowly and breaks our enthrallment. "Dude, I'm hearing strange noises, and I'm not kidding this time. We should leave."

Jack looks at me, and I nod in agreement.

"Okay, give us a minute," he says to him.

Sam gives us a knowing gaze and gets back in the car.

Jack fixes my panties and skirt, then zips up his jeans. "Are you ready, baby?" he asks with a gratified smile. I nod yes.

He steps out of the throw and wraps it around me. He hugs me tightly, gives me a long kiss on the lips, and then lightly spanks me.

"Let's go," he whispers in my ear.

CHAPTER 28

Inside the car I take off the throw and set it on my lap. Jack's turned on the heat, and I decide my hands have a much better use. I place one on his leg, so I can run it up and down as I please. We have a long drive off this mountain, and my hand on his leg should help keep him alert.

"Dude, want me to drive?" asks Sam.

"I got it, thanks," replies Jack.

Of course he does, my strong, self-sufficient, resilient man. I smile at him, blissful that he's mine.

He leans over and whispers, "Keep your hand on the prize, baby. I need to stay awake." He gives me a brief kiss on the lips and starts the car.

I'm trying to stay awake, but it has to be well

past 4:00 a.m. Jack must be exhausted. That thought helps keep my eyes half open and my hand on his manhood.

Marie and Sam are passed out.

This time of morning, traffic is very light, and we make it home in record time.

"Do you want to stay over?" I ask.

We're parked outside my place, and Sam and Marie are still sleeping in the back seat. I'm hopeful he'll say yes, so we can finish what we started on the mountain.

"Baby, your hand's been on me all this time. If I stay, we won't sleep, believe me," he kisses me.

My belly is yearning with desire for him.

Then stay!

"And we have that voter registration thing in," he checks his iPhone, "two hours."

"What!" I retort, eyes wide.

"Baby, it's 7:00 a.m.," he chuckles, grabs my hand, and kisses it.

"Hmm, I don't know if we're going to be there by 9:00."

"We may be a little late," he jokes. "I'll call you to wake you."

"That's okay. You sleep and don't worry about me. We'll be there," I assure him.

"I'd pick you up after, but I promised my dad I'd have dinner with him. Will you be okay getting home?" He's caressing my cheek.

"Of course, I'll Uber it, since Marie is heading to a concert."

We kiss again, and then I wake up Marie and Sam.

෨෨෨

The alarm is buzzing. I keep touching the snooze, but the damn thing won't stop. It goes off again, again, and again!

Fucking piece of...

"Crap, Marie!" I shout, as I realize why the alarm's been going off.

It's 10:00 a.m., and hell, I feel horrible! A sleep hangover is so much worse than an alcohol one.

I drag myself to Marie's room and nudge her, until I wake her. She can barely open her eyes.

"Get up, we're so late. I'm going to take a quick shower."

"Okay, wake me when you're done," she replies woozy and closes her eyes.

An hour later, I text Jack.

Ellie: Hey sweet baby you there yet? We're just leaving
Jack: You're sweet
Ellie: Yea but you're HOOT!
Jack: LOL! I'm a Hoot?
Ellie: Funny! Hooooottttttt... My hottie!
Jack: And you're MINE!
Ellie: Damn right!!! 🖤

Ellie: We're so late

Jack: Lucky there are 3 other peeps there

Jack: Do you know your location?

Ellie: No Marie's dropping me off. I think Mike texted
her the location

Jack: He didn't text you?

Ellie: Nope. She says I'm in WeHo

Jack: Ok good

Ellie: What's your location?

Jack: Near UCLA

Ellie: Careful with all those hotties 😈😈😈

Jack: Hotties what hotties...

Ellie: Jack...

Jack: Ellie...

Ellie: 😊😊

Jack: I only have eyes lips and hands for you!

Ellie: Good ditto! 😊😊

Jack: Be good baby don't fall asleep on the job

Ellie: LOL! TTYL baby

Jack: Remember I'm having dinner with my dad I'll
text you after xoxo

Ellie: Yep xoxo

෨෨෨

On the way to my station, we stop to pick up coffee
for ourselves and the six other souls that we're
sure made it to their post on time. Maybe they'll
forgive us, if we come bearing gifts.

It's noon when we finally arrive at my post in
West Hollywood. Marie drops me off and heads
back to her station closer to home in Century City.
She'll only be there until 3:00 p.m., and I will
finish the day at 5:00.

The three other people at my station are great, and don't give me any grief for arriving late. I tell them I had been working on a "special project" until 7:00 a.m., and they all praise me for actually making it to this event.

"I would've totally ditched this thing, if I were you," a blonde with a valley accent says to me.

If she only knew my "special project" was getting mind-blowing finger-love from Jack, at the peak of Mount Baldy.

Freaking best night ever!

It's a beautiful, sunny LA day, and while at times I feel like taking a nap, other times I'm thoroughly entertained by my colleagues' approach with people. They're super friendly with random people, as they explain the importance of registering to vote.

I stick to handing out the registration cards and pens and filing the signed ones. I'm in no shape to small talk with anyone — I'm afraid I'll fall asleep mid-sentence.

૭≈૭≈૭≈

It's finally 5:00, and I'm ready to get the Uber, head home, and sleep until tomorrow. That's my plan anyway, but something makes me look up from my iPhone, and I see Mike approaching.

What the hell is he doing here?

"Hi," he grins at me, like he's my boyfriend here to pick me up after a long day at work. "You're done? How was it?"

"Yea, it was good. I hope I helped. I'm just getting an Uber to head home," I reply, flabbergasted to see him.

"No, I'll take you home."

What!

I look at him bewildered, and he makes an attempt to explain himself.

"I thought I'd come by and pick you up," he says, leaving me more confused than before.

"Why?"

"I mean, you don't mind if I take you home, right? No big deal," he shrugs, as if picking me up is the most natural thing for him to do.

I want to bark at him, *"Ah, yea, it's a big deal! Until not too long ago, you weren't even speaking to me. In fact, you were being a total asshole walking away every time you saw me approaching, you fucking rude SOB!"*

But I'm too tired to waste my energy on someone who means so little to me, and hell, he's going to save me the Uber fee.

"Okay," I follow him to his car.

He's smiling at me, genuinely smiling like the nice, charming Mike I once knew.

"I just have to drop these documents off at my office. Do you mind? It'll be a quick stop," he checks with me.

I shrug and continue following him.

I'm quiet most of the ride. I have no idea what this is, what to make of it, or what to say to him. Does he want to be friends now? Does he want me back or something? He doesn't stand a chance. I love Jack. Why the sudden change? Maybe he's bipolar, and he's finally on meds. I smile at the thought.

He parks outside his office in downtown LA. "I'll be right back," he leaves me to wait for him.

My house is completely out of the way from his office. This is quite a detour. What is up with him and this new accommodating, cheerful Mike?

He's making small talk on the way home, asking me about work and how I like living in LA. I'm giving him the bare minimum. I'm polite and civil, but I'm not giving him an inch. I don't want him to think I'm still interested. If Jack thought I was, it could ruin things.

Jack, shit!

Should I tell him Mike drove me home? It'll piss him off, for sure, even if he doesn't say anything. What if Mike mentions it to him? What if he doesn't? Maybe this odd incident will remain just a ride home. That's all it is. It's probably best not to say anything.

I text Jack as soon as I walk in the front door.

Ellie: I'm home miss you 😘

Jack: Ditto baby

Jack: Just arriving at the restaurant

Ellie: Ok enjoy

Jack: I'm going to be thinking of you

Ellie: Me too A LOT!

Jack: Sweet things or dirty?

Ellie: DIRTY!

Jack: Tell me more...

Ellie: You, me, the front passenger seat of your car...

Jack: 😍😍😍 MORE!

Ellie: Kissing, touching, thrusting, hard...

Jack: Mmm I'm so turned on!

Jack: Fuck I want you!

Jack: Shit! My dad's here

Jack: I'm ditching him and going to get you!

Ellie: 🐻😚 Jack be nice

Jack: LOL!!!

Ellie: 😂😂😂

Ellie: Talk later. I'm taking a little nap... Like till
       tomorrow morning

Jack: LOL! Ok baby dream of me loving you

Ellie: Always! Hope you get home soon and rest

Jack: Yes baby

Ellie: My hottie!

Jack: Damn Ellie what you do to me!

Ellie: 💋😜😘

I fall asleep without a care in the world.

CHAPTER 29

I've caught a cold, probably from my co-worker Eva. I tried to stay away from her, but we share an office, and it didn't take much to catch the virus. I've called in sick, and I'm staying in bed to nurse this illness. I'm taking advantage of my idle time and grab Marie's iPad to finish *The Power of Now*.

My body aches. I'm taking vitamin C and cold medicine, hoping I can get rid of this inconvenient ailment soon.

I reach for my cell that just pinged with a text.

Jack: How's your day going baby?
Ellie: Fantastic I'm in bed
Jack: What, why, with who?
Ellie: A cold please don't interrupt our affair
Jack: LOL! You don't feel well?
Ellie: Just a minor cold

Jack: I can go take care of you
Ellie: 😊 Thank you but I'm ok
Jack: Sure? We can play doctor
Ellie: Hmm tempting 😊 but I don't want you to get sick
Jack: So...
Ellie: I'm fine. I'm cozy in bed and I'll be ok in a couple of days
Jack: Xoxo baby!
Ellie: 😵😷

⁙⁙⁙

I haven't brushed my hair or washed my face all day. What's the point? I'm too tired and achy to do anything but stay in bed.

I'm grabbing a glass of ginger ale, when the doorbell rings.

It's probably that delivery Marie is expecting.

I open the door and see Jack.

"Hi, baby," he smiles.

I gasp — *Hell, I look horrible!*

I shut the door on him.

"Ellie, open the door," I hear him laughing.

"Sorry," I plead. "Give me two minutes," I shout through the door.

I run to the bathroom with new found energy. I brush my teeth and wash my face. In my room, I apply tinted moisturizer to give my pale skin a bit of color, comb my hair into an acceptable pony tail, and change into a clean pair of PJs.

This will have to do.

I open the door, and he's leaning against the doorframe, smirking, holding a large paper bag. He moves to walk inside, but I block his way.

I stand in front of the door with my arms crossed, smirking back at him.

"What are you doing here?" I bite my lip.

"I'm here to take care of you," he replies cheerfully.

"I thought we agreed I was okay." I'm desperately trying to hold back a happy, jubilant smile, because I love that he's here.

"You agreed. I didn't. Are you going to let me in?" he stares me down with his piercing bluish-gray eyes.

"Depends," I banter.

"On what, Ellie?"

Damn, he's hot!

"On what's in the bag."

"Chicken noodle soup," he says, trying to stifle his laughter.

"Hmm, that's a mighty big bag for chicken noodle soup."

"And orange juice and bread," he explains sweetly.

"Bread, huh?" I arch one eyebrow.

"Fresh, *warm* bread," he gives me a concupiscent grin.

I smile back and throw my arms around him.

He almost drops the bag on the floor.

He leans in to kiss me, but I turn my face away.

"I don't want you catching my cold," I explain.

"I'm a strong man, Ellie, I can take a little cold," he grabs my face with one hand, turns it to him, and plants a loud kiss on my lips.

He commands me back to bed, while he finds tableware. I do as I'm told, because he's just too cute to resist.

"Open up," he instructs. He's feeding me soup in bed.

"You know, I can feed myself," I say, after the third spoon full. "I do have the strength to *spoon*," I tease.

He laughs and quips, "I sure hope so. We'll get to that later. First you eat, open up."

I happily do as he says.

&ﾟ&ﾟ&ﾟ

We're lying on the bed, my head on his chest and our arms around each other.

Marie walks into my bedroom, and she immediately stops when she sees us.

"Huh, well this is interesting. What's up?" she crosses her arms and grins.

"Jack came over to take care of me."

"I see. Is he doing a good job?" she asks amused.

"Yes," I smile and squeeze him.

"We're watching a movie. You want to join us?"

She takes a few steps inside and looks at the TV. "The Notebook?" she mocks, lifting an eyebrow.

I give her another smile and Jack shrugs.

"Damn, Jack, you're a goner!" she declares and walks out, shaking her head and laughing.

He rented The Notebook and Love Actually on iTunes. I'm pretty sure he had never seen either before tonight and hadn't planned on it. But he thinks it's the type of movie I want to watch, and it proves to me how much he cares.

What he doesn't know is that Love Actually is one of my favorite movies of all time, but I will tell him, so he knows how happy he's made me.

Jack always makes me happy.

He was just what I needed when I was most broken. I don't know who or what intervened, but I thank them from the bottom of my heart for bringing Jack to me.

CHAPTER 30

Jack's been here all day. It's late. I wonder how much longer he's staying. I don't want him to go, but I also don't want him to catch my cold.

"More orange juice, soup, water, anything?" he asks sweetly.

"No, baby, you've fed me enough, thank you," I giggle, delighted he's in bed with me. I'm wrapped around him, my head resting on his chest.

"Are you laughing at me or with me?"

"Both," I respond playfully.

"Both?" he looks down at me and tilts my face up to him with his finger.

"You're way too adorable, you know that?" I say, loving his inquisitive eyes on me.

"I don't want to be adorable. I'm strong, manly,

and tough," he grunts.

"Okay, now I'm really laughing at you," I smile and kiss his chest.

"What do you want, Ellie?"

"Hmm, water maybe," I say, not understanding what he's asking.

He scoots down so we're face to face and just stares at me. His eyes are intense, eager, gripping...

"No, *what* do you want?" he asks again.

I search his eyes for what he's refusing to tell me.

"You," I reply, studying him.

He remains quiet, but his beautiful bluish-gray eyes are bright.

I'm going to say it again, but I sneeze instead, so loudly and forcefully, I almost bump him on the head.

"Sorry," I cover my mouth mortified.

He chuckles.

"Are you laughing with me or at me?" I ask embarrassed.

"Both," he replies. "You really *are* adorable, Ellie, and I want to take care of you. Can I stay?"

"Yes," I say, but quickly add, "but you shouldn't, because I don't want you to get sick."

I try to pull away from his embrace, so he knows I'm serious, but he holds me tighter.

"You said you want me, now you have me, baby, cold and all."

"But..." Before I can finish objecting, he removes my hand from my mouth and kisses me on the lips.

"Jack, don't. You can stay, but don't kiss me," I reprimand him.

"Well, that's a first, a girl asking me not to kiss her."

"What? Who else have you been kissing?"

"You have a cold, baby, and my lips need to be kissed on a daily basis," he teases.

I try to escape from his embrace again, because his answer stings, even though I know he's kidding.

Hell, I hope he is kidding!

He won't let me go.

"Jack's got the ladies eating out of his hands," Mike's snide comment overpowers me like a tsunami, sending my fears into high gear.

"Well if you're out there kissing other girls, I suppose I should find someone else to kiss too."

"You want me to go then?" He asks smiling.

"Yes," I push him away again. This time he lets go and peers at me, amused.

"I'm glad I amuse you," I sit up crossing my legs and point to the door.

I sneeze again hard, my nose runs, and I don't have a tissue. Self-conscious and mortified, I wipe it with my hand, like a child.

Without another word, he gets up and walks out the door.

Crap, how did this game go so wrong, so fast?

I'm freaking out. If I go after him, I'll look like a fool. If I don't, I'll be a fool. It's a lose-lose for me either way.

But he walks back in holding a box of tissues. I let out a breath I didn't know I was holding.

Thank you, baby Jesus!

"Here," he says, takes a tissue out of the box and wipes my nose. Then, he takes my hand and cleans that too. After he's done, he pulls me up to him and wraps his arms tightly around my waist.

"I'm not going anywhere, even if you *are* kicking me out," he emphasizes.

"You said you kiss other girls," I fuss.

"I said you have a cold, and I need my lips to be kissed every day, which means cold or no cold, I'm kissing you."

"Oh!" I pout.

"You pout a lot," he teases. "And it's fucking sexy, because I want pull that tasty lower lip of yours," he leans in and whispers in my ear.

Mmm, yes, PLEASE!

"Now bed. I'd prefer my beautiful girl get well sooner rather than later," he kisses me softly on the lips. "And don't you *dare* kiss lips other than mine," he warns and spanks me lightly, making me yelp.

"You like to spank me, don't you?" I observe smiling, climbing back in bed.

He undresses, amused, and gets into bed next

to me. I snuggle to him, my arm around his waist, and my head on his chest.

"It's not a spank, baby, just a light touch when I need to get your undivided attention."

"You always have my undivided attention. I kind of bite a little," I confess shyly.

"I've noticed," he smirks.

"I want to take a real *bite* out of you," I leer up at him.

"I'd love for you to take a bite out of me too, as soon as you're better," he chuckles. "Right now you need your rest."

"Okay. Just don't go around kissing, spanking, or whatever, other girls," I say, recalling the memory of him with that "friend."

"Baby, I haven't kissed anyone else, since the first time I kissed you," he says. "And I should've probably kept that tidbit to myself," he mumbles quietly.

"Thank you for telling me," I kiss his chest softly.

"I hope you haven't either," he says with trepidation.

"Nope," I reply immediately and playfully bite his bare chest.

"Mmm," he grunts.

"Love bite," I say.

He's turned on. I can feel the tension in his body, but he won't make love to me, not tonight.

He's here to take care of me not do me, though I wish he would.

My hand is on his abs, and I'm aching to run it up and down his entire, hard, muscular body. I want to trace his abs with my tongue and nibble at every inch of him.

Mmm, if only I wasn't so revoltingly ill.

I'm sure I can motivate him to give up his good intentions, but my runny nose reminds me how disgustingly sick I am. Besides, I really don't want that aching, throbbing, thrusting — well, I do.

Gah, stop Ellie!

I don't want him to get sick, basically.

"I have to leave really early in the morning, baby," he interrupts my reverie. "I won't wake you, so you can rest. I'll text you and come by later in the day to check on you."

I nod okay, and he kisses my forehead.

"Good night, baby," he reaches for the side lamp and turns it off.

"Good night," I kiss his chest again, but I can't help myself and bite him.

"Mmm, Ellie!"

"I know, sleep," I whisper.

I sense he's smiling, because I am. I do as I'm told and fall asleep peacefully in his arms.

I wake up with a smile plastered on my face, but it quickly dissolves when I notice he's gone. I had hoped to watch him dress, but I missed the show.

I reach for the note he left me on the nightstand.

"It was my turn to watch you sleep. I love taking care of you, thank you for letting me. Your Jack."

CHAPTER 31

"I got it, I got it!" I scream, jumping up and down in the living room.

Marie walks in and jumps up and down with me. "What'd you get, what'd you get?" she asks laughing.

"The editor position at Music & Radio Today magazine," I hug her and shake her from side to side.

"You go girl!"

I can't wait to tell Jack. He's the first person that comes to mind any time I have good news. He's going to be so thrilled and proud of me. I'll tell him in person tomorrow.

But amid this happiness, one thought vexes and confounds me...

Why didn't I confirm my stay in Los Angeles, when Angela Richards offered me the job? Why did I hesitate?

"You're staying in Los Angeles for sure, then?" she asked.

"Can I have a few more days to confirm?" I requested.

She agreed.

Why do I have doubts? Is my subconscious warning me, reminding me to get all my ducks in a row before making a final decision?

Jack and I have a conversation pending. I love him, more than I can even express. I believe he loves me too, but has he *chosen* me? Has he chosen me definitively?

I can't wait any longer. I have to talk to him. We can't have any ghosts lingering around us, not Mike nor any of his girl "friends," not if we want to have a chance at a real life together.

Maybe we can talk tomorrow. I'll start with the good news about the job, and then find a way to bring up the rest. I'm anxious at what he might say, but I have to talk to him.

෨෨෨

"Wait!" Marie is standing in front of me, stopping me from exiting the front door.

I'm dying to see Jack. I haven't touched him since a few days ago, when I was sick.

Why is she stopping me?

"Why? What's going on?" I frown at her.

"Mike's here, with Jack and Sam," she replies soberly.

"What!" Good thing they're all outside and can't hear my stupefied tone.

"I don't know why Mike's here, but he's coming with us," she examines my mood.

I've entered an alternative universe.

What is he doing here? What is his end game?

I stare at her for what seems hours, until she grabs my arm. "Put on your best smile, and get out there. You're not going to let Mike ruin your night," she stresses.

She's right...damn right! I pull myself together and head out with her.

Mike tagging along means nothing. I'm Jack's, he's mine, and we're going out together. Mike can do whatever he wants.

Jack is standing by the driver's side of his car, Mike by the passenger. They're talking to each other. I'm expecting Jack to come greet me, to kiss me, and claim me. But he just looks at me and doesn't move.

Mike notices we're here, and turns to us smiling.

"I'm joining you. I hope you don't mind."

What the hell is this?

Shit, Jack is hiding our relationship again.

He's looking at me with trepidation.

Don't do this again, Jack!

Then a cold chill comes over me...

Did Mike tell Jack he drove me home, after the voting registration event? Crap! If he's upset, he should come to me, have faith in my love for him. I've done everything I can to prove to him that I love him, that I want nothing to do with Mike.

My breathing gets heavier and faster, as agitation and disappointment grow inside of me.

Jack wants to play, let's play!

"Not at all, it's so nice to see you," I smile broadly at Mike, touch his arm, and kiss him hello on the cheek.

I give Jack a scornful, mocking smile. That's what he deserves right now. He looks back at me with panic and regret.

Mike opens the back passenger door for me, and I get in, before Jack has a chance to say or do anything.

I'm so distraught, and everything around me seems cloudy. I don't even notice that Marie is with Sam in his car, until we're on the road, and I receive a text.

Marie: How are you?

Ellie: 😒
Marie: Shit!
Ellie: Jack has a lot of explaining to do!
Marie: Yea he does!
Ellie: What the hell Marie! Why am I here in this
        situation?
Marie: Breathe just breathe. We'll figure it out

Mike informs me we're making a stop to pick up a friend. I wave him off. I don't have time for his nonsense.

I'm looking down at my iPhone. I can't look at Jack, because I'm afraid I'll see all of his imperfections, all of his fucking uncertainties about us, and I will begin to hate everything I love about him. There will be no turning back from that.

Ellie: We're going to pick someone up a friend of
        Mike's I think
Marie: Wait what?! Let me check...
Ellie: At least that's what I think he said
Marie: Ellie it's not Mike's friend it's Jack's

I can't type a reply.

My fingers won't move.

My body's entire energy source is suddenly at my throat, where an ocean of tears has amassed, and is threatening to choke me.

I refuse to let the tears make their way up to my eyes. I clear my throat over and over.

We arrive at an apartment complex in Studio City and wait.

Jack and Mike get out of the car to say hello to the girl who is obviously Jack's date. Mike opens the front passenger door for her, and he sits in the back with me.

I will not cry, I will not cry, I will not cry, FUCK, I WILL NOT CRY!

She says hello. I return the greeting, smiling as best as I can. I don't look at her for long.

Mike is next to me, and I decide neither of these two fools is going to break me.

"Is that the new iPhone?" I ask Mike.

What a trivial and idiotic thing to ask, but my brain is fried with indignation.

Idiotic will have to do.

"Yea, here," he smiles and hands it to me.

"I have the previous version," I show him, holding both iPhones in my hands.

"Are they really that different?" I engage him so he moves closer to me, hoping to really piss off Jack.

He deserves it!

"Not by much, here I'll show you," he takes his iPhone and scurries even closer, so close that my arm is touching his.

This is the Mike I knew, the guy with a heart who was once attentive and sweet. How things have changed. Despite his reprehensible behavior, I don't hate him, though I certainly don't love him anymore. I would rather it was Jack sitting back here with me.

Mike and I are almost comfortable with each other, but that's all it is. Anyone looking in from the outside would assume we're back together. They'd be wrong, but maybe we can be friends one day.

Jack floors the gas, startling us.

"Careful," I meet his gaze in the rearview mirror. "Precious cargo on board. *Your* precious cargo in the front," I hiss at him with contempt and get back to Mike.

I don't look at him again. I concentrate on Mike. I don't want to hear anything she's saying to him or his response.

To think that some days ago, he was in my bed taking care of me. I can't wrap my head around it. Why does he do this? He's my perfect, loving Jack one minute, and the next, he's doing everything in his power to ruin things.

CHAPTER 32

We're at a house party in the Hollywood Hills. I don't know anyone here and neither does Marie. Who the hell decided to come to this random outing?

Ugh, how infuriating!

Jack finds a place a few feet away from the rest of us and settles there. He looks distant, detached, and dejected.

It's his fault!

I don't want Mike, I love him, and yet he seems to be saying, "Go ahead, Mike. She's all yours. Take her back. I don't care!"

Not that I'm entirely convinced that's what Mike is after. He just wants to make sure everyone knows I belong to him, because apparently he has no clue

I've moved on. And Jack isn't getting in his way. Why? Is he scared of Mike? That can't be it. Jack can take him, easily. But if Jack isn't afraid of Mike, then what is it? Why isn't he standing here with his arms around me, his lips on mine, letting the world know I'm his?

"You want to try this?" Mike offers me his drink.

"No," I respond harshly and walk away. I've worked myself into a fury. All I want is to be out of this purgatory.

"Muñe, calm down," Marie puts her arm around my shoulders and pulls me aside.

"I know, but I feel like kicking Mike in the balls and decking Jack," I growl.

She giggles, "Well, you can take them for sure."

"Why is Jack doing this? One day we're great, the next he's bringing Mike and a 'friend' on our date. How fucked up is that!" I laugh loudly, because it's better than crying.

Marie hugs me. "Look," she says, eyeing Jack.

He looks miserable.

Despite my resentment and anger, I can't resist him. I walk over to him, not giving a crap that his "friend" is nearby.

He's mine! He may not claim me, but I claim him!

I stand in front of him feeling uneasy but hopeful, all at the same time.

Your move, Jack...

He gives me a warm, caring smile and hands me his drink. He seems relieved that I'm making an effort. I take the glass, take a sip, and hand it back to him. We do this, our thing, not saying a word, just gazing at each other. It's just him and me, together.

It's not long before Sam announces we're leaving. We haven't been here more than an hour or so, but none of us are having a good time.

I'm riding in the back seat with Mike again. It's fucking awkward. I'm so peeved at Jack. I swallowed my pride and disappointment. I made the first move. I approached him tonight. I *chose* him. He could've chosen me too. He could've told her and Mike to fuck off. He could've led me to the front seat of his car to ride with him, but he didn't. That speaks volumes.

We drop off Jack's "friend" at her apartment. He says goodbye to her, but we don't leave immediately. Mike steps out of the car and joins Jack to talk.

Marie and Sam were following us in Sam's car, and as soon as they arrive, Sam joins Jack and Mike.

They're standing several feet from either car, far away enough that neither Marie nor I can hear their powwow.

What are they discussing?

Ellie: What the hell are they saying?
Marie: No idea. It's the strangest night ever
Ellie: Seriously!
Marie: Sam said you were rude to Mike
Ellie: Cause I didn't take his drink? Mike's done
      worse to me. Screw him...them!
Marie: That's what I said. How are you doing?
Ellie: At a breaking point!
Marie: Hold on we'll be home soon
Ellie: If these fuckers hurry up
Marie: LOL!
Ellie: And why am I still in this car? I'm going with
      you so Jack and Mike can be happy together
      since they love each other so much!

I'm opening the car door to get out, when Jack
and Mike get back in. Jack turns on the car to
leave.

Damn it!

Ellie: Missed the window of opportunity
Marie: Don't worry we'll be home soon
Marie: Are they talking to you?
Ellie: No and they better not. Fuckers!
Marie: LOL!!!

Mike is messing with the radio and settles on
an Oldies Spanish station.

*This night is getting more bizarre by the
minute!*

I start softly singing along to the radio.

Ellie: Shit I was just singing a song and now Mike's

going think it's about him
Marie: Which one?
Ellie: Selena the one about hoping deep in your soul
he'd stay forever then he leaves so now you can
only be friends
Marie: No me queda más?
Ellie: Ugh yes!
Marie: Shit stop singing!
Ellie: Duh I did!

I giggle at our exchange.

I'm glad the boys are hearing me laugh. I don't want their last image of me to be of a distraught Ellie.

I never imagined Jack would treat me this way, but apparently, I was wrong. They've both seen me at my worst, and I won't give them the satisfaction ever again!

We're close to home, and I'm ready to end this icky night once and for all. I'm going to need a long shower to wash off the stench of this evening.

I jump out of the car as soon as we arrive home.

"It was nice seeing you, Mike," I kiss him on the cheek good night.

"Bye, Jack," I wave quickly, and don't wait for him to come around the car to kiss me goodbye — not that he was going to anyway. He's lost that right, at least for tonight...maybe longer.

"Bye, Sam," I shout at him, while I'm opening the front door to the house. I blow him a big kiss with my hand, letting one special finger protrude.

I was rude to Mike, huh, Sammy. Here's an extra goodbye for you!

I'm in the kitchen picking at a muffin and making coffee, when Marie joins me, giggling.

"Did you just give Sam the middle finger?" she asks, amused.

"Maybe...but it wasn't just for him, it was for all of them. I'm done, Marie. I'm so done with this shit!" I reply distressed.

She stops laughing, "Ellie!"

"I am. I was planning on having a conversation with Jack tonight to tell him the good news about my new job, but I also wanted to finally ask him to make a decision about us. He just made that choice without saying one word. I guess actions do speak louder than words."

"Ellie, you have to understand the situation," she tries to calm me down.

I interrupt her.

"Yea, the code we broke. I get it. But I also know I can't be in this position forever. Mike will be his friend forever. I once loved Mike, and that fact is part of my past. It will never change, ever! And frankly, I wouldn't change it if I could, because you were right. I do thank Mike for leaving me. He forced me to grow up. And because he left me, I met Jack, even though I very much dislike him at the moment. Mike gave me Jack. So whether Jack makes a decision now or later, he will have to make one. And everything he's doing is telling me that he's choosing Mike's friendship over me. It hurts like hell, but it's okay."

Marie is silent. One of the few times she's not trying to convince me of this or the other. One of the few times she doesn't have some quick advice for me.

She knows I'm right.

"You know my new boss asked me to confirm that I am staying in LA. I asked her to give me a few days let her know for sure. Who does that? This happened yesterday morning, Marie. Yesterday morning my gut was telling me to leave my options open. My intuition was reminding me that Jack hasn't chosen me, that he's not completely mine. I may be going to New York," I sigh sadly at the realization that Jack and I may be over.

"Ellie, you can't just go. You have to talk to him, tell him what you're telling me. He may not deserve it entirely, but please do it for yourself," she pleads.

"Yea, I'll sleep on it. I promise. You want to do something fun tomorrow?" I ask, because I don't want to dwell on today any more.

She's bemused. She was expecting me to spend Sunday in bed crying. That's old school Ellie.

My cell pings, and I know it's Jack.

I ignore it.

My heart is aching because of him, and right

now, I can't handle reading or hearing his excuses. Not tonight.

CHAPTER 33

I've always thought The Grove is one of the most beautiful shopping centers in LA, especially at night. During Christmas, it's like stepping inside a movie, and you can't help but be joyful.

Marie and I are spending this beautiful, spring Sunday there. We've chosen to have lunch at the Farmers Market. I love that place. It's so inviting, and the food options are varied and always delicious.

The plan is to do some shopping, window shopping at least. I've always been fascinated by the assortment of designer shoes at Nordstrom. If I could only afford them — I will one day. Right now, it doesn't hurt to browse and try on a few pairs just for fun.

My iPhone is off. It's been off since last night, and I like it. I feel unhindered. I have a lot of thinking to do, important decisions to make and I will...starting tomorrow. Today is just for me and my best friend to enjoy a beautiful day, without any distractions or upsetting reminders.

I have no worries about having my cell off. My family knows that if an emergency comes up, they can always reach me through Marie. Jack knows it too, but I've warned her I don't want to know if he texts or calls.

I need a break from him, from his misgivings, from my disappointment at his unwillingness to fight for me.

Why can't he tell Mike once and for all that we're dating? I suppose I should try to understand his position, but I've given him enough time. I've put up with his "now we're on, and I'm yours" and his "now we're just friends, and I'm showing up with another woman" to prove it.

It's not my fault Mike invited himself on our date. Jack should've said no and set the record straight about us, but he didn't. I won't know why until I speak with him.

❧❧❧

It's early-evening when Marie and I walk back to the Farmers Market for dinner, after spending hours trying on shoes at Nordstrom.

The warm, spring breeze softly caresses my cheeks, and it feels comforting. I stop, look up at the sky momentarily with my eyes closed, and take a few deep breaths to fill my lungs.

I suddenly feel the urge to run.

I look at Marie with a smile, "I'll race you," and take off like a pro runner — good thing I'm wearing sneakers.

I glance back at Marie, her 5'3" frame chasing after me, huffing and puffing. "Not fair," she squeaks. "You have longer legs."

I stop near the entrance to the Farmers Market, out of breath, clenching my stomach, and laughing. She catches up a few seconds later, breathing heavily and smiling. From the look in her eyes, I sense she's wondering why I ran. I don't know exactly why — I'm not particularly fond of running. I think I just needed to exorcise some of the stress that's been building inside me, since last night.

That felt good!

Marie finally catches her breath, and we walk straight to Pampas Grill for a delicious churrasco.

With our plates overflowing with meat and salad, we sit and watch people stroll by as we enjoy our food.

She's giving me that please-don't-be-mad look she always gives me, when she's about to break the rules. I sense she's aching to ask me about Jack.

"Spill it, Marie. I know you're dying to ask me something."

"I am," she giggles nervously. "Why did you love Mike?" she blurts out.

Not what I expected at all!

I stare at her a few minutes pondering, unsure how to answer.

"You don't know?" she prods.

I decide to come clean.

"When Rob flew me to New York, the weekend after I confronted Mike, one of his last pieces of advice was to stop fretting about the break up just because I had nothing better to do."

"Wait, he thought you loved Mike because you were bored?" she interrupts, surprised at what I just said.

"No, silly," I laugh. "But he had spent the entire weekend listening to me go on and on about Mike, questioning why he left me, what I had done wrong, hearing me complain about how I would never love anyone like that again, blah, blah, blah, and he had had enough. He wanted me to be honest with myself and realize that I didn't want to let go of Mike, because it was easier to live obsessed in a tortured fantasy world, than face reality, and open my heart to new possibilities. You know why? Because doing so would have taken effort, self-love, and guts. Deep down, I always knew Mike wasn't mine, that we weren't a good fit," I take a deep breath, as I realize the depth of my own admission.

"I loved Mike because he's good looking, he turned my life upside down, and it was exciting. I loved him because he wasn't entirely available, and it allowed me to live in a fake-fairytale relationship. I loved him because his bad-boy, detached approach appealed to me. I loved him because in those rare moments, when he let the walls down and opened his heart, it felt like heaven. I loved him because sometimes love is irrational, and I still had some growing up to do. What can I say?"

"Wow, I just opened Pandora's box," she exclaims giggling.

I laugh with her.

"Not quite," I reply. "But you asked, and I was ready to answer."

Her second question, I wasn't ready for.

"Why do you love Jack?" she eyes me timidly, hoping she didn't just ruin my mood by bringing him up, when I asked her not to. But I'll bite. Maybe talking about it will help me put my feelings in order.

"Because he's *fucking HOT!*" I peel my eyes at her. "Every...Single...Inch...of Him is Delicious!"

She laughs and practically chokes on her food.

"I can agree with that," she says, after she's regained her composure.

"He is *hot*. He's beautiful, damn beautiful!" I

take a deep breath and continue in a more serious tone. "But that's just the wrapping. Jack saw me when no one else did, when I was so broken, I couldn't even see myself. He stuck with me, when he didn't have to. And when those bluish-grays look at me, when he touches me, kisses me...It's everything! When we're together, he makes me feel like the sun shines just for me, like the earth is spinning simply because I exist, like the galaxies are within my reach. We haven't made love yet, but just thinking about what it would feel like when his mouth is on me, when his hands are tracing my body, when the warmth of his love overruns me...in that moment of pure, unadulterated passion when we're finally entirely skin to skin..." I stop, sigh, and shiver.

I have to stop my train of thought before I combust.

"As gorgeous as he is on the outside, he's all substance on the inside. He's loving, caring, kindhearted, spontaneous, funny, determined, strong, and smart as hell! He treats me like I'm his priority — despite his most recent actions," I say sadly, because the thought of him with *her* burns inside my soul. "I have a million reasons to love him," I finish and smile, feeling gloomy and uneasy.

"So give him a chance to explain," she appeals.

"I will, but I need time. I need time to arm myself with the strength to withstand whatever he says to me and to be strong enough to walk away, if I have to. I need time, Marie, just a bit more time."

"You can't walk away, Ellie. He's your Prince Charming, your *happily ever after*," she implores, pulling at my heartstrings.

"I agree, but he has yet to choose me. I have to be prepared for every scenario. I love him enough to understand that. I will speak with him, I promise, just not today. Enough about Jack and Mike!" I beseech her.

"Yes," she replies and pretends to zip her lips with her fingers, locks them, and throws away the key.

I smile satisfied that this conversation is over and get back to my food.

❧❧❧

We're home late, with just enough time to shower and prepare for tomorrow's work day.

I turn my iPhone back on, because I need the alarm to wake me up in the morning. The screen immediately lights up with notices of missed texts and voicemails.

I ignore them.

They'll have to wait, especially if they're from Jack.

I'm handing in my letter of resignation at the record label in the morning and only giving them a few days' notice, because I may end up moving to New York. If I do, I need extra time to prepare for the move. If I don't, I can still use a few days to meditate and work on me.

But first things first...sleep.

CHAPTER 34

Today was my last day at the record label, and I've said my goodbyes to Dan and all of my new friends. I'm now looking ahead, hopeful at the amazing possibilities that await me in my new job at M&R Today.

Only one thing is hanging over my head: I have to talk to Jack. My cell has been blowing up the last couple of days. I suspect it's all him. But I've been too confused and disappointed to bother checking.

Sometimes I muse about leaving to New York without ever speaking to him again. I get over it seconds after I think it. It's immature, and I would end up hating myself if I did such a selfish thing.

Even though I'm hurt, I know I have to speak

with him. I won't read any of his texts nor listen to his voice mails. I need to speak to him with a clear head and a clean slate. I have to do it for me, for my own peace of mind. I don't want to move on, if that's what it comes to, without giving him the opportunity to choose me. Mostly, without telling him how much I love him, how much I choose him.

That conversation has to happen today. The sooner I know where Jack and I stand, the faster I can move forward with my life. It's best to rip off the Band-Aid in one swift pull. Maybe it will hurt less.

I promise myself to have an open heart, take a deep breath and text him.

Ellie: Hi Jack can you stop by the house today?
Jack: Please tell me you're ok, I've been trying to
**   reach you since Saturday night**
Ellie: Yes I'm good
Jack: Have you read my texts heard my voicemails?
Ellie: No sorry. Can you come by?
Jack: You hate me
Ellie: No
Jack: Have I lost you?
Ellie: You're not being fair
Jack: I'm sorry
Ellie: Are you?
Jack: Yes

This is too much, too intense to discuss over text.

My heart is aching, so I get to the point.

Ellie: 6pm good for you?
Jack: It's that bad
Ellie: I'll see you at 6?
Jack: Yes
Ellie: Thank you

∾∾∾

Marie walks in the living room, where I'm preparing to receive Jack. She's examining me, waiting for me to look at her. I haven't told her he's coming over, but she knows something's up.

"Does Jack know the editor job is a done deal?"

"No," I reply, as I'm setting the wine and glasses on the coffee table.

"Are you telling him tonight?" she continues.

"Yes."

"Is that what the wine is for?"

"Yes."

"He's coming over, then?" she grins at me.

"Yes."

"That's a lot of yeses, Ellie," she nips. "Just a few more questions. Are you telling him you can choose to stay in LA or move?"

I nod yes.

"You don't want to discuss it?" she asks, her arms folded.

"No," I eye her nervously.

"Well, do you want another bottle, or *two*, of wine?"

I gape at her and try not to laugh at our strange exchange.

"If I discuss it with you now, I'll lose my train of thought and my nerve. I don't know how this is going to go down. I'm still upset with him for bringing a *friend* to the house party. I don't know why he'd think that would be okay with me. I don't know why he would risk our relationship like that. I have so much riding on this one conversation, I just..."

"It'll be okay, Ellie. Just be honest with him. Don't hold back. This is Jack you'll be speaking with, not Mike," she tries to reassure me.

"I know," I concede, but I can't help how nervous I feel.

I'm startled by the doorbell.

He's here.

CHAPTER 35

"Hi," I welcome him with a kiss on the cheek. *I promised to have an open heart.*

"Hi," he kisses me back, his eyes full of anxiety.

"Hey, Jack," Marie breaks the ice. "See you later, Jack," she waves goodbye and leaves.

"That's a quick getaway. Is she okay?"

"Yep, she just has things to do. Come in. Wine?" I offer.

We sit on the sofa next to each other. My pulse has skyrocketed. This is me, no barriers, no armor, no holding back. Me, an open heart and a naked soul in front of the man I love, hoping he feels the same way.

"I have great news," I say, taking a sip of wine to try to calm my worried heart.

He smiles, his lovely eyes watching me carefully, waiting to hear what I have to say.

"I've been offered the editor position."

"That's awesome, Ellie!" He's excited for me and reaches for my hand to kiss it.

I let him.

He doesn't let go.

"And I can choose to be based out of LA or New York," I continue.

"What do you want to do? Do you want to go?" he frowns and grabs the wine glass from the table to take a drink.

"I don't know," I respond, because my decision depends on his answers.

"I have until the end of the week to decide, then another week to make the move...if that's what I choose to do." I swallow, searching his eyes for a clue to what he's thinking.

He gives me nothing, so I press.

"Do I have a reason to stay, Jack?"

His frown deepens, and he releases my hand.

No!

"That's something you have to discuss with Mike," he answers acidly, leaves his wine glass on the table, and stands.

His words slap me like a cold, hard hand.

"Why would I do that?" I ask, affronted and confused.

This again? Why?

"He's the reason you're having trouble deciding, isn't he?" He sounds unsettled and irate.

"Why would you say that? Mike and I have been over for a very long time. But you and I..." I'm stumbling over my words, thrown for a loop by his unwarranted comment. It's hurtful.

"What are you saying, Jack?" I shake my head trying to organize my thoughts. "I thought you knew how I..."

"How you *what,* Ellie? Mike has been very clear every time he's told me you will always be his," he says with a dry tone.

"Wait, what?"

When did this happen?

"I don't know anything about that, Jack. I don't know what it means, or why Mike would say it."

"But it's important to you, isn't it?" he says, wounded. "You like that he thinks of you that way."

"Of course not! How can you say that, after all he's put me through? I thought you knew...I thought you knew how I feel about you," I implore, hurt by his reckless accusations.

"How *do* you feel, Ellie? I distinctly remember you unwrapping yourself from my arms as soon as Mike saw us together. You dismissed me. And I think deep down maybe I always expected you push me aside for him. But fuck, when it happened, it..." He doesn't finish the thought and closes his eyes, as in pain.

His account of that night is like a kick to my gut.

I can barely breathe.

He's letting me know just how profoundly I've wounded him, when all he's ever wanted to do is love me. I did this to him. I put doubt and fear in his mind. I pushed him away. I can't defend what I did, but I can try to explain it.

"Jack, what I did was wrong. I'm sorry! You have no idea how much I regret that moment."

I place my glass of wine on the table, stand, and reach for him, but he instinctively steps back. I put my hands down, feeling rejected.

How do I make him understand?

"I was confused back then. I was still broken and scared. I was scared of letting you in, of allowing you to care for me, of allowing myself to care for you. But in the time we've spent together, you've changed all that, you have given me so much," I try desperately to explain myself.

As I'm pleading my case, his demeanor changes, hardens. He stands taller and crosses his arms, essentially putting up a wall between us. I sense his next words are going to bury me.

"I'm not your second choice, Ellie. I'm not the one that *saves* you from Mike. I hurt too. I bleed too. I can't go there with you, because you can end me. You have that power."

I can see he's hurting, and I don't know how to

make it stop!

"That's the last thing I want, Jack. You can end me too," I confess, tears pooling in my eyes.

I'm aching to touch him, to hold him, to show him how much I love him. But I hold back, afraid he'll push me away again.

"You're not a second choice. Please forgive me, if I've ever made you feel that way," I implore, tears rolling down my face.

"You've never fought for me the way you fought for him," he utters, cutting me deep. "I know you confronted him that night he left the wedding. You wanted him back," he hisses between his teeth.

"So much has changed since then, Jack. I have fought for you. I was fighting for you every time you showed up with a *friend*, and I didn't say anything, even though it killed me. You wanted to show me that you can easily replace me. And I swallowed my pride and let you have your vengeance, because I had hurt you first," I wipe the tears from my eyes and take a deep breath, trying to keep some level of composure.

"Despite them," I fist my hands and close my eyes briefly, because I need a second to erase from my memory the image of him with those other women.

"Despite those girls, I always felt like I was the center of your world, or so I thought, and it gave me a reprieve from the bite of your payback," I confess.

"*Despite* them? You should have fought for me, Ellie! I've been waiting for you to fight for me the way you fought for him. Yes, you *are* the center of my world. I wish I could have hidden it better, but it's written all over my face. Mike sees it too, and he's drawn a line in the sand, and I just can't cross it," he says heatedly.

"You can't or won't?" I ask, desperation in my voice.

"I can't. Not if you don't fight for me," he mumbles subdued.

"I am fighting, Jack, I've been fighting, I'm fighting now," I reach for him, my hands fisting the sleeves of his white shirt.

He doesn't move.

"I'm not a possession Mike can claim as his. I'm the girl he discarded. He left me and that voids all claims. He's not part of my life anymore. He doesn't own my heart, Jack. You do. I love you!"

I want to pull him closer, but his entire body is stiff, heavy, like a statue nailed to the floor. There's nothing I can do, until he decides differently.

CHAPTER 36

"I don't think you'll ever love me the way you love him," he confesses.

And there it is!

I finally know the root of everything, of why he doesn't show me affection in front of Mike, of why he doesn't tell him about us, of why he unexpectedly shows up with other women.

It's a test, a metric to measure my love for him. It's his way of safeguarding his heart. If he retreats just at the right moment, if he holds back when he's getting too close, I can't rip it out of him.

I'm sure Mike's deceitful words have confused him even more. I don't know when they spoke, or what ridiculous garbage Mike said to him, but he succeeded at his goal.

He's planted a seed of doubt...

I don't recognize the Jack standing in front of me. Mike took my Jack away, and replaced him with a phony version that's bathed in his damn insecurities.

"Loved, not love," I correct him.

"Jack, the thing about love is that it's unpredictable. We never know how or when it's going to find us. It can slay us or strengthen us. It can be gut-wrenching and butcher us, make us bleed and push us to our breaking point, until we're dwelling in the darkest, filthiest, most dreadful part of our soul. But once it's done, once we learn the lesson it's trying to teach us, if we pay attention, it will reward us.

"I removed the veil from my eyes, Jack, and I paid attention. I learned my lesson. Maybe I don't deserve it. Maybe it's too soon. Maybe I have more dues to pay. But somehow, for reasons beyond me, the universe saw fit to reward me now. It showed me the beautiful, generous, honest, fulfilling, candescent side of love. Its true self...with you."

The lump in my throat is choking me.

I swallow trying to clear it, because I have to ask him the end-all question.

His answer will determine my immediate future.

"Do you love me, Jack?"

This is it.

I wait for his response, holding on to his shirtsleeves.

His darkening now-gray eyes are blurry with unshed tears.

Answer me, Jack, please, answer me...

I love you!

He closes his eyes and solemnly says...

"I don't know."

My world instantly shatters.

It appears New York is a done deal.

I have to love him enough to let him make this choice.

I have to love myself enough to let him go.

I have to be strong enough to take care of me and heal, far away from him.

Maybe I'll be able to face him again, once I don't love him so much, but right now, I can't stay.

When he opens his eyes, I see his anguish.

He's chosen his friendship with Mike over me. The chips fell on Mike's side, and he's won once again.

"You're asking me to fight for you, Jack, but you have to be willing to fight for me too. But you've made your choice. I hope you find that grand love you deserve. I really do wish that for you, because I wish that for me too. Goodbye, Jack," I say desolately and reach up and kiss him gently on the cheek...one last time.

CHAPTER 37

I've left him alone in the living room, but right now, I just need to tend to my wounds.

As I'm heading to my bedroom, I hear the front door close.

Marie peeks out of her bedroom, and her face falls when she sees my tears.

"What happened?" she follows me in.

I sit on the corner of my bed and recount the entire conversation, while she's pacing and shaking her head.

"It's over. New York sounds exciting," I say dimly, wiping my tears.

"You're both idiots!" she shouts. "You're letting your egos and fears get in the way, and ruin things. Why can't you just admit you love each other?

You're both crazy as fuck...and meant for each other!"

"What?" I say between sobs.

"Come on, Ellie, you're crazy for each other. I mean, cray-cray for real!"

"He said he doesn't know if he loves me, Marie. What more is there to say? I'm not doing a Mike here. I'm learning from past mistakes and letting go," I whimper.

"Wait, so Mike you chase home, pound on his door, and confront him. But with Jack, the guy you're clearly supposed to be with, your real Prince Charming, you just give up on?" She's perplexed and outraged. "I'm starting to think Jack's right. You're not fighting for him. You're running away instead," she accuses.

"I'm not running," I defend myself sobbing. "I'm learning from past mistakes. Marie, I asked him point blank if he loves me, and his response was, 'I don't know.' How much clearer do I want it? To quote Sam's blunt observation: Do I need a neon sign on his forehead letting me know it's over?"

"You choose now to quote Sam's idiotic comment," she sneers. "Fuck, Ellie!"

"I need to call the magazine to let them know I'll be moving to New York, then make arrangements with Rob to stay with him, until I find my own place," I say dejectedly, because my only option is to move full speed ahead. I have to keep my mind busy, until I'm across the country away from Jack.

"New York, then?" she glares, sadly. "You can stay here, Ellie. Don't run."

"I'm not running," I repeat in my defense. "I'm trying to protect myself, to do better, and grow up. Staying here means seeing Jack and Mike more often than I care to. They're still your friends...our friends. They do have a way of showing up in our lives. It's for the best, Marie. I'm tired, exhausted of fighting first for Mike and now for Jack. It's time I fight for me. It's way overdue."

She shakes her head and hugs me, because that's all she can do for me.

⚘⚘⚘

Rob's thrilled I'm moving to New York, and I want to live with him for a while. But he's also worried about what's happened with Jack. He thinks Marie is right, that I should stay and fight for him.

Neither he nor Marie understand how awful Jack's "I don't know" felt. Mike's non-answer to why he left me was shitty but Jack's feels worse. It feels definitive.

I can't stay. I won't stay to be haunted by what could've been. I did that with Mike for far too long and lost myself in the process.

"You can stay with me as long as you like. We'll

be roomies forever, if that's what you want. You're my sweet girl, my best friend, and I love you more than I can express. I'll make sure you have fun things to do day and night. I'll definitely introduce you to some very charming, successful men. Count on it! But I think you belong with Jack," says Rob.

"I love you, Rob, forever, but this is the last time I'll allow you to say that to me. It doesn't help me. Jack's made his choice. There is absolutely nothing I can do about it. What I can do is move on. I can find my life somewhere else, have a great career, and heal my heart, so that it can eventually be open and receptive to a man that's ready and able to love me the way I deserve. Maybe I'll even learn not to fuck it up," I laugh, trying to find some humor in this tragedy.

He exhales sharply. "Okay, Ellie, I won't mention it again. Just make sure you're one hundred percent positive you've done everything you can. No regrets."

I roll my eyes, frustrated. I've been getting the same nonsense from Marie.

"I have. I told him he owns my heart, and he said he doesn't know if he loves me. End of story."

I can't take any more of this, it's draining.

I make an excuse to end the call.

"We'll talk later, sweetie. I have a lot of planning and packing to do. See you soon, love you," I hang up.

Rob and Marie don't understand why I'm not pining around crying for Jack like I did for Mike. They think I've given up, that I'm unwilling to fight for him, maybe even that I don't love him enough.

Losing Jack will mark my life forever. A year ago, I would've said it was Mike who owned the most important period of my life; who owned my heart. I was addicted to him, but like any addiction, it was unhealthy and destructive.

I'd like to think I've grown up a bit since then. Jack's love gave me a natural high and taught me how to love myself, because he was always there for me, despite everything, despite everyone. But his "I don't know" ruined it.

I can survive without Jack, not because I don't love him, but because I do. I know what I want now, what I'm willing to accept and not accept in my life. I've gotten here, in part, because of him.

That immature, ego driven man, who's afraid to love because he doesn't love himself, is not someone I want in my life anymore.

I choose a man that's warm, loving, affectionate and kind, a man with an open heart who sees me. I choose Jack. Well, someone like him, because he doesn't love me, not enough to fight for me.

Losing Jack is the hardest thing I will have to endure, of that I'm sure. He deserves more than a miserable, pitiful, hopeless mess of a girl unable to let go. He loved me too well. His love built me up

so high, breaking down is not an option.
    With Mike I was lost.
    With Jack I found myself.
    Now, a new life awaits me in New York.

CHAPTER 38

I just have a few more things to pack, my flight is booked, and I'm almost ready to head to New York.

It hasn't been an easy past few days. Jack has not left my mind. Not one day, not one hour, not one minute, not one second.

As sad as this end is, I also have a lot to smile about. I will always remember the absolutely fascinating things we did. He took me to the top of a mountain at dusk. I'm sure no one else will ever do that for me again.

I suppose he can take his next girlfriend there.

Hell, maybe that's his thing.

I hope not.

I choose to think he did that just for me.

I mentally send him my best wishes every time I think of him, because that's what you should do when you love someone.

க்கைக்கை

I'm taking a break from packing, and watching a random documentary on Netflix, not really paying attention. Truth is, I just need noise to distract me.

Marie walks into the living room and stands in front of me, blocking my view of the TV.

She's scowling.

Something's happened.

"What's up? Why the face?"

"I have something to show you," she broods.

"Okay..." I caution. "What?"

"I'm only showing you because I think you should know, not to upset you," she warns.

"Okay..." I repeat, intrigued and getting a little worried.

She shows me her iPhone. "Jack's been texting me asking about you."

"For how long?"

"For days. I've gotten four texts in the last few seconds. He's starting to annoy me."

"What does he want?"

"To know how you are, when you're leaving, if you're okay. Take a look," she hands me her phone.

Jack: Is she ok?
Marie: Who?
Jack: Marie!
Marie: What do you care!
Jack: Please
Jack: Just tell me she's ok
Marie: She's ok
Jack: You're lying
Marie: Maybe
Jack: Don't be mean
Marie: You're mean to put it politely... Burn!
Marie: Leave her alone you got what you wanted
Jack: What do you mean?!
Marie: You won't see her again... Ever!
Jack: What! What do you mean?!?!?
Marie: Go to hell Jack! You told her you don't know
        if you love her deal with it!
Jack: What do you mean I won't see her again?!
Marie: She's moving to NY thanks to you!
Jack: She can't leave!
Jack: Tell her she can't leave!
Marie: Why would I do that? It's your fault she's
        leaving!
Jack: Please Marie!
Marie: 🐑🖕🍫!!!
Jack: Fuck!
Jack: At least tell me how she is
Marie: That's none of your business anymore!
Jack: Tell me!
Marie: Ugh whatever Jack!

I glare at her, mildly amused. "How many texts are there? You've been going back and forth with him like this?"

"Yep," she nods.

"You're just taunting him..."

"He deserves it!" She giggles, clearly proud of herself.

"What do the latest ones say?" I ask, while I scroll down.

> **Jack: Marie please tell me when she's leaving**
> **Jack: Waiting...**
> **Jack: Answer me!**
> **Jack: Fuck! Fucking answer me!**

"Damn, he cursed at you!" I bite my lip, trying to suppress my smile.

I'm excited he's thinking about me, that I'm still on his mind.

She giggles, "Yep, that's why I didn't answer him. Besides, he really wants to hear from you. He should be texting *you*, not me...If he had the balls!"

"Marie!" I shake my head at her.

"I know he's *your* Jack, but I can't solve his issues. He has to do that on his own," she teases.

"Answer him," I plead with her.

"You answer him," she counters.

"But it's your phone and he texted *you*," I narrow my eyes at her.

"Ellie, you do know that if you answer him, he won't know it's you touching the little keys on the screen to make words, right?"

"Duh!" I roll my eyes. "But I still want *you* to text him back," I hand her the iPhone.

"You're as bad as he is. Like I said...made for

each other." She shakes her head in mock disbelief.
"Text!" I command grinning.

Marie: She leaves in a couple of days
Jack: How is she?
Marie: Same as yesterday same as the day before
Jack: Doesn't tell me much
Marie: Too bad...

I'm next to her eyeing her answers, amused.
He's so adorable.
An idiot for rejecting me, but adorable!

Jack: I need more
Marie: I'm sure
Jack: Please Marie
Marie: What!?
Marie: Is she crying for you? No!
Marie: Has she stopped eating? No!
Marie: Is she dreaming of you? No!

He doesn't reply immediately...
Finally, three minutes later.

Jack: Does she have a place in NY?
Marie: Yes
Jack: Where?
Jack: With who?
Marie: Her true love

"Stop antagonizing him!" I give her a playful
shove.

"I'm enjoying this too much not to," she laughs. "Stop!" I finally laugh openly.

Jack: Fuck Marie!
Marie: Duh! With Rob
Jack: Good
Marie: And his gorgeous roommate

He doesn't respond, and I'm done watching this cat and mouse routine. I can't deny I'm elated that he wants to know about me, but it's a trap.

If I give his texts any credence, I will trap myself in a cycle of hope. Hope that he'll come back to me. Hope that he'll tell me he loves me. Hope for a future. I can't afford the uncertainty of the hopeless hope that's starting to brew in my heart, after reading his texts.

Marie is right, if he wants to know about me, he should text me, he should be here talking to me, holding me, kissing me.

Stop, enough, Ellie!

"I'm going to take a shower. It's late, and there's no point to this. Like you said, if he really cared, he'd be talking to me," I say discouraged and turn off the TV.

"I didn't say *if he really cared*. Of course he cares! Otherwise he wouldn't be annoying me with so many questions."

"Maybe," I sigh. "I'm taking a shower." I get up from the sofa and begin to walk away.

"What do you want me to say to him when he replies?" She calls out after me.

"Whatever you want," I shrug and motion with my hands that I don't care.

CHAPTER 39

The warm water feels relaxing on my face. My eyes are closed and all thoughts drift to Jack.
God, I love him.

Who would've thought I'd be here, after that first time at Sonny McLean's, saying wholeheartedly: I LOVE JACK MILIAN!

But I have to let him go, because even though he's asking about me, he won't fight for me, not against Mike's nonsensical claims.

He won't admit he loves me, but I think he does. It comforts me to believe it.

It will take me a long time to get over him, but I'm hopeful one day I will. He will be the one I measure all men against.

The shower door flies open!

"What the hell!" I'm startled.

I turn and see Jack. His eyes are blazing with determination.

Am I dreaming?

My heart is pounding so hard out of my chest by his presence that I forget my nakedness.

"What are..." before I can finish, he steps into the shower fully dressed, grabs my face with both hands, and kisses me urgently.

His mouth invades mine, his lips pull and tug at mine desperately, begging me to let him love me. It takes me a nanosecond to realize this is not a dream, and Jack is really here.

His hands move to my back and crush my naked body to his. He places his forehead on mine and exhales sharply, "My Ellie."

I'm holding on to his shoulders. I want to stay in his arms forever, but I can't.

"No!" I push him away.

I take a deep breath and cross my hands over my chest to cover myself.

"What are you doing here, Jack?" I demand.

How dare he do this to me! He can't disturb the little peace of mind I have.

He's drenched, the water revealing every contour of his delectable body underneath that wet, white shirt. The captivating sight of him is distracting, so much so that I almost overlook my anger.

I catch myself and scowl at him, protecting myself from him, because one right word, and I will be his for good.

"Don't hide your body from me, Ellie," he pleads, reaches for me, and holds me by the arms.

I plant myself strong, so he won't be able to move me. But I know that one swift pull, and I'll be in his arms.

"Answer me, Jack. What are you doing here?" I try to shake his hands off me.

"I need you, baby. Please let me stay," he pulls me into an embrace.

His words almost do me in, but before I let him stay, I need to know what this is. I can't let my heart hope, if he's going to walk away later. I love him, more than he actually realizes, but I will not let him, or any other man, yo-yo his way in and out of my life anymore.

I want all or nothing.

If he won't give that, I will kick him out for good!

"You need me now?" I breathe into his chest, where my face is happily resting.

"Yes," he replies.

"Do you want me?"

"Yes," he repeats.

"Just for today?"

He realizes where I'm going. He tips my face up to him with his fingers, examines me with yearning and reverence, and kisses me slowly on the lips.

"Today, tomorrow, and every day after. I don't make sense without you, Ellie."

"Are you sure, Jack?" I stare at him.

"Yes."

"I can't do this. I *won't*. Not if you're unsure, if you're going to walk away again," I say firmly, gazing into his eyes, trying to hide the fear eating me up inside.

"I'm sorry I walked away from you. I'm so sorry," he pleads. "You're the oxygen I need to breathe. The thought of not being able to touch you, to love you is asphyxiating me. The thought of you with anyone else tortures my crippled heart. I've been dwelling in the pits of hell without you. Save me, Ellie. Please love me again. Let me love you," he implores.

"I've believed you so many times, Jack. Then you pull away from me," I say, anguish in my voice.

"I'm sorry, baby, I'm sorry."

"That's not good enough," I gaze into his worried eyes. "I won't allow you to play with me again, to hurt me, to slay me, no matter how much I love you."

"Slay you? Baby, no!"

"That's what you do to me every time you walk away, Jack," I confess with tears in my eyes.

"No," he closes his eyes and holds me tighter, horrified he's hurt me so deeply.

"Do you love me?" I ask expectantly.

"Yes!" He opens his eyes and kisses my wet lips.

"Do you choose me, the way I choose you, against everyone and everything?" I need an absolute answer.

"Yes, baby, I do!"

His bright bluish-gray eyes tell me he's not lying, that he loves me as much as I love him, that he's choosing me. I see him, and he finally sees me. The uncertainty is gone, this time for good.

I throw my arms around him and kiss his titillating lips, which I've been missing so much.

I have my Jack back!

We hear Beyoncé's "Drunk in Love" playing loudly, invading the entire house.

It's Marie's doing.

He smiles, and I giggle at her timing.

"How the hell *did* this happen? Because I *am* drunk in love with you, baby," he words on my lips between kisses.

The soft kisses morph into deep, needy, carnal desire. His lips are all consuming, pleading for forgiveness for lying when he said he didn't know if he loved me.

The torment that's been building inside me since I heard him say, "I don't know," the exhaustion and anguish piling up inside my soul thinking I'd lost him are too much to contain inside my vulnerable heart. And I let out a deep sob between his whispers of, "I love you, Ellie, I love you."

I hold him as tightly as my arms can muster, because I never want to let him go. He can feel my ache, my need for him, and his lips are making sure I know I own him as much as he owns me.

Yearning, frantic desire is taking over us. He pins me against the wall, one arm wrapped firmly around my waist, his other hand nestled in my hair, cradling my head, and his mouth is venerating mine. My hands are in his hair, holding on tightly, and all I can think is, "He's mine!"

I take a breath and look at him. I put my hands on his chest and begin to unbutton his shirt. I'm trying to move as quickly as my clumsy fingers can manage.

He watches me with lascivious desire, while I work the pesky little buttons.

Finally! I slide the shirt off his arms and toss it on the floor. I run my lips over his naked chest, leaving tiny kisses as I go, a dust of his hair softly tickling me. Then I trace the outline of the muscles of his arms with my index fingers.

He's watching me intently, his hands around my hips pulling me stalwartly into his erection.

Mmm, I can't wait!

I move my hands to his chest again and slide

my index finger down the middle of his abs. Then I take a detour to trace that V that leads me to the button of his jeans.

He's staring at me, grinning, but doesn't move. He's letting me do as I please. His jeans are bulging tight. I lick my lower lip in anticipation, as I flick open the button and pull down the zipper. I sneak one hand inside his boxers and grab his impressive erection.

"Mmm," he groans. "I crave you so much, baby," he whispers

I move my hand to pleasure him. I've been here before. I'm excited to be here again.

"Stop," he says suddenly.

What? No!

He takes my hand out of his boxers and pulls my hips into his bulge again, kisses my cheek, and whispers in my ear, "Bed. I'm going to love every inch of you, Ellie. I'm going to take my time savoring you, pleasuring you, like you deserve."

He starts to nibble at my earlobe, sending tingles through my body. "And I don't want us to break our respective necks in this shower," he spanks me, making me yelp.

I look at him turned on and excited. The fire inside me is scorching.

Please hurry up, Jack!

"Okay," I manage to say.

He reaches behind me to turn off the shower,

then fastens his hands around my long hair and wrings out some of the water.

Grabbing a towel, he orders, "Arms up." I do as I'm told, and he wraps it around me. Then he takes another towel and gently runs it through my hair.

We step out of the shower, and I hear a squeak. I look down and notice he's got his sneakers on — *he ruined one expensive pair.*

"I was in a hurry," his glorious lips twisting playfully.

"It looks like it," I pun delighted.

He bends down and removes them, along with his socks, while I step toward the vanity to search for condoms.

"I've got it covered," he says, guessing what I'm looking for. "I came here determined to love you, Ellie, hoping you'd let me."

"Of course you did," I fire back, grinning.

He grabs my hand and walks me to my bedroom, as Ed Sheeran's "Thinking Out Loud" accompanies us.

I look up at him. "I think we're going to have our own soundtrack the entire night. Thin walls," I smile.

He grins back and winks at me.

Thank you, Marie!

৵৵৵

We're standing in front of my bed. I try to remove his jeans, but the wet material isn't cooperating. He places his hands on top of mine and helps me push them down, along with his boxers. He steps out of them, pushes them aside with his feet, and wraps his arms around me. His hands are on my behind, but I keep mine in front of me.

I have big plans for them.

He kisses me passionately, and I take his erection with my eager hands and massage him up and down, soft and hard, until he moans on my lips.

I make an effort to kneel to take him in my mouth, but he stops me.

"Please," I beg.

"Later."

He takes off my towel, tosses it, and lays me gently on the bed. "I need to taste you first, baby," he whispers, "and love you like you've never been loved before. Love you like you belong to me, like I belong to you!"

He lies on top of me, his legs on either side of mine. He's holding himself up by his elbows and is gazing at me. His beautiful bluish-grays are full of love...and regret. Regret that he left, regret that he didn't tell me he loves me, regret that he almost lost me.

I take his face with my hands and stare back at him. I kiss his lips softly, over and over, while Camila's crooning "Todo Cambió."

"You hear that, even the universe knew you were mine," I whisper.

I need him to know that I am only his, that no one will ever mean more to me than him. I need him to know we're okay.

No more regrets. No more doubts.

He finally smiles, kisses me gently on the lips, and shifts, so only half his body is on top of me.

"Get ready, baby," he says and burrows his face in the apex of my neck, kissing it, then my throat, my shoulder, my chest, until he reaches my breast, and settles on my nipple. He's suckling my right nipple, and his fingers are circling and pulling at the left one, making me moan.

Holy shit!

His mouth continues suckling, but his hand follows a downward path through the middle of my chest, stomach, and down my pelvis, until he finds his goal. He slips two fingers inside me and begins circling, thrusting, pressing slowly then fast again and again, torturing me deliciously.

My hands are in his hair, holding on tightly, keeping him in place so he can have his filling of my breast. I moan louder and louder, between muffled cries of his name.

My Jack is here, with me, touching me, savoring me, loving me. I've waited so long for this, to feel his fully naked body on mine, to have him in my bed making love to me.

I'm in rapture.

The feel of him, his exuberance, the intimacy of his mouth on my breast, the feel of his fingers invading me again is unlike anything I've ever felt before. It's my first time, my *real* first time being loved with this intensity, with this reverence, and with this kind of unrestrained love.

And he's all mine!

My body tenses, my legs tighten, and I explode screaming, "Ahh, Jack!"

I'm breathing heavily, elated and satisfied he can love me so much.

He gives me a quick respite, while he puts on a condom. He hovers above me and tenderly kisses my forehead, one cheek, then the other, the tip of my nose, and lastly, my lips.

He looks into my eyes. "I'm going to have you now, baby. I'm going to make you mine. You hear me, *mine.* I'm going to bury myself deep inside you, so you can feel what you mean to me. And I'm never letting you go," he says, as he penetrates me in one quick, delicious thrust.

He's inside me, where I've wanted him to be, where I've yearned for him to be for so long. I'm relishing every delicious inch of him.

He's filling me, stretching me, claiming me.

He feels divine, heavenly, hard, and tight inside of me. I feel his warm, labored breath on my neck, where he's buried his face.

My legs are wrapped around his hips, my arms around his neck, and my fingers are digging into his back. He's thrusting, hard, fast, urgent, claiming me over and over.

I'm holding on to him for dear life, sucking and biting his shoulder, trying to quiet my loud moans. He's going to have a vampire bite tomorrow, but I don't care. He's mine to bite if I want.

He pulls me up so I'm straddling him. His mouth is on my nipple again. "Move for me, baby. Show me how much you want me," he commands, between suckles.

"How much I love you, Jack, love you!" I correct him. "I'm yours!"

I feel his smile on my breast.

He grabs my hips and moves me to his rhythm. It's so deep and intense. I'm riding him fast, hard, deep, voraciously.

My love, my Jack.

"Ahh, mine," I moan. "I love you. Love me, baby, please. Don't ever stop loving me. I need you...mine," I mumble incoherently and suck on his shoulder again, hard, as the pleasure is racing throughout my entire body.

"Yes, baby, always," he pulls at my hips harder, so I can feel him deeper inside me.

"Mmm, you're so warm inside..." he moans. "Feel me, baby. Take me, hard," he commands. "This is what you do to me. I'm yours, Ellie. Yours!"

he grunts.

Hearing him is enough to bring me closer to the edge. We're both close, very close.

I thrust my hips to push him deeper inside me, and I can't contain the swirl of emotions overtaking me. I come loudly screaming, "My Jack!"

Happy, gratified tears roll down my face.

With one more, heady push inside me he finds his own release. "Yours, baby!" he groans.

He's still inside me, holding me in place. We look at each other, and he notices my tears. He gazes at me with inquiring eyes and wipes them with his thumb.

"They're happy tears," I promise him.

He smiles and kisses my forehead.

We're breathing heavily, sated, and blissful in each other's arms.

We've both wanted this for far too long, but there was always something in the way. We always found reasons not to make love. The timing wasn't right yet. There were too many fears, too many ghosts between us. I'm glad it happened now, when we truly belong to each other.

CHAPTER 40

He's on his side facing me, our legs entangled, and his hand is playing with mine.

He's studying me with apprehensive eyes.

"I love you, Ellie," he reassures me.

"I love you too."

"I don't want to lose you. You are *my everything*. I'm not going anywhere, I promise. How could I? I don't have a future without you. You're my reason to be, to dream, to hope, to soar. I exist for you, Ellie. Please believe me," he implores.

I'm staring at our fingers twist and turn, like they've done so many times, listening closely. I let him say what he's wanted to say from the moment he burst into the shower.

"I'm sorry I said I didn't know if I love you. I

lied. I was scared. Not of Mike or losing his friendship. I was scared you could never love me the way you loved him," he looks at me with longing.

"But when you said those things about love, I knew you were right, but I had already fucked up so badly. And when you said goodbye, my world ended. I felt lost, adrift in a daze, because I had ripped out my own heart by letting you go. I realized I'd rather have you, even if you loved me half of what you loved him, than not have you at all. I felt like a fucking punk for not fighting for you, for not holding on to you. I don't think I've ever been in so much pain, Ellie. It was torture, baby."

This is quite an apology and confession, if I've ever heard one.

"Say something, please."

"You have my heart, Jack," I gaze into his eyes. "You put it back together and strengthened it. You own it, and it's yours to do as you please. You can safeguard it, or you can rip it to pieces and cripple me for life. I'm at your mercy. Does that convince you?"

"But you chose to leave. Would you have left him too?" he sulks.

I sigh heavily.

It worries me that he keeps bringing up Mike.

"Please don't make any more comparisons," I kiss him and gaze into his expectant eyes. "My love for you is intoxicatingly blissful, it occupies even the most microscopic space in my heart," I sigh. "It's everything and more. Mike's love, or lack of, weakened me. Yours strengthens me. That's why I'm able to leave, because I love you, not because I don't. So please don't bring him up again."

"You're still leaving, then?" he asks sadly.

"Do I have a reason to stay?"

"Yes, baby. Me, because I love you," he replies forcefully, like he needs to get his answer in before a deadline expires. "I want you to stay. I need you to stay and be mine, be my best friend, my girlfriend, my lover, my wife," he takes my hand and kisses it sweetly.

His wife...Yes, I'd like to be his wife one day.

"Am I expecting too much from you?" His eyes are guarded, waiting for my response.

"No, you're not, Jack. But I also need to know *you* are mine, *only* mine!" The thought of him with those other women still hurts and vexes me.

"You have my heart and soul, Ellie. Of course I'm only yours. I've always been yours, from the moment I first kissed you, maybe even before."

He moves on top of me, hovering, propped up on his elbows. He kisses me softly on the lips again and again and smiles, that glorious smile that belongs only to me.

"Now that that's settled," I giggle, "What made you come running over here?"

"Marie," he grumbles, and turns on his side again. I do the same, so we're facing each other.

"Of course. What devilish deed did she do?" I run my fingers through his soft, wavy hair.

"It's what she texted me," he quips. "She said you were moving in with Rob and his tall, hot, rich roommate, who was thrilled to meet you because you're just his type. And he had Rob's stamp of approval. The perfect guy for the perfect girl," he rolls his eyes, amused but annoyed at her audacity.

"You know she was lying, right? There's no roommate," I grin, admiring his luscious lips twisting in ire.

"Everything went dark when I read her text. I was pissed and scared. I knew I had to get you back. I got in my car, drove like a madman, stormed in here, and jumped in the shower."

We're both laughing at Marie's antics, while Ricky Martin is singing "Perdido Sin Ti." I reach for him and hum the melody on his lips.

"Mmm, perdido sin ti," he replies on my lips and eagerly proceeds to lick, suck and kiss every inch of my body, just like he promised.

My skin is over sensitized, and now Chris Isaak is going on about "Wicked Game."

Hmm, time to torture him...

I push him on his back and straddle him.

"My turn to be wicked...with my mouth," I warn him. I grind my hips against his erection, so he knows where I'm headed, and start my exploration down his body kissing, licking, sucking, and biting.

"Holy fuck!" he groans.

CHAPTER 41

I wake up to Jack spooning me, one of his hands on my boob.

Even asleep he loves them.

I turn slowly to face him, careful not to wake him. There's a trace of a smile on his lips. My heart swells with joy.

Damn, he's beautiful, and he's mine...finally.

I want him again, but we've barely slept all night, and my limbs are aching from all the exertion. I slip out of bed carefully, and put on my PJs. I grab his boxers and jeans from the floor. They're still quite damp. I empty his pockets, so I can put them in the dryer, and he'll have something to wear when he wakes up.

Crap, his iPhone is in his back pocket — *that's*

a goner!

I pick up his shirt and socks from the bathroom and head to the kitchen to grab something to drink.

Marie's sitting at the table having breakfast.

"Good morning," she says, not even trying to hide her devilish grin.

"I'm just getting some orange juice," I smile at her, "and putting these in the dryer." I show her his clothes.

Why do I feel so shy?

She clearly knows what was going on. She instigated the entire thing, so he'd come running over.

I'll have to thank her later.

"Rough night, huh?" she teases.

"You could say that."

I can't look at her. Our bedrooms are wall-to-wall, and I'm sure she heard every moan, groan, and scream.

"Thanks for the soundtrack," I walk to the dryer, place his clothes inside, and turn it on.

"You're welcome," she mocks. "I figured I should muffle the noises, if I wanted to sleep."

"Did you?" I ask, as I'm making my way to the fridge to grab the juice.

"A bit," she puns.

I'm mortified.

I'm glad the orange juice is at the back of the fridge, so I can hide behind the door for a second longer. I'm kidding myself. She's is still there, teasing me with her mocking grin. She must've heard everything.

"I didn't hear anything," she puts me out of my misery. "Aside from blasting the music near our mutual wall, I had my headphones on, listening to my own playlist."

"Oh," I twist my mouth relieved.

"I just heard, 'Jack!'" she screams, laughing.

"What!" I laugh too, because the neighbors down the street probably heard me as well, music or not.

☙☙☙

I sit with her and catch up, until Jack's clothes are dry, but I don't eat, despite her offer to make pancakes. I want to wait for Jack.

The dryer buzzes. I take the clothes out, grab the glass of orange juice, and head back to my bedroom. Marie follows me.

When I open the door, I see Jack's awake with his back resting on the headboard, his arms crossed. He looks beautiful but worried.

He grins when he sees me, and before I walk in, I catch Marie asking me quietly, "Is he awake?"

I nod yes.

"Good morning, Jack!" she screams. "You're welcome, Jack!"

He laughs at her outburst.

I walk in and close the door behind me. He's pensive, and it frightens me. I place his clothes on top of the dresser, crawl back in the bed, and kiss him gently on the lips.

"What's wrong?" I ask. We had such an amazing night. I hope he's not having doubts again.

"Your iPhone is soaked," I inform him and point at the nightstand.

"Yea, I didn't think about that one," he replies distracted.

"Is that why you're so worried?"

"Ellie, I'd destroy a million iPhones for you. Come here," he reaches for me.

I move closer to him and hand him the glass of orange juice. He takes a drink, places the glass on the nightstand, pulls me until I'm leaning against him, and embraces me.

"If you want to go to New York, you should go," his lips are against my hair.

"What!" I look at him perturbed and frightened at what he's implying.

"It's not what you think, baby," he regards me. "I don't want to hold you back. If New York is where you can reach your career goals, we can do the long distance thing, until I can move there with you."

"No, Jack, no! It won't work!" I reply distressed and alarmed.

"I'm not Mike, Ellie."

I narrow my eyes at him, as soon as he says it.

"What I mean is we *will* make it. I will move to New York with you in time. I just need a couple of months to settle my businesses here," he explains.

"Please don't bring him up again. And no, I'm not going!"

"Ellie, I promise..."

I put one finger on his lips to quiet him, so I can finish what I have to say.

"My boss would actually prefer that I stay. She was being very accommodating about the move to New York, but I'm sure she'll be thrilled when I give her the good news that I'm staying. She has been dropping hints here and there about making LA my base. Believe me, she'll have no problem with the change, and my career won't suffer. I promise."

"Are you sure?" he frowns, examining me.

"Yes, believe me. I will be saving them a lot of money by staying in LA. Plus, I wouldn't go now anyway," I smile and kiss him. "But seriously, it's all good."

"Okay, good," he smiles and hugs me tighter. "God, I love you, Ellie. I'm one fortunate SOB."

I kiss him again. I want to jump him right this second, but he still looks anxious. I undo his embrace and straddle him. I need to look at him in the eyes to figure out what's going through his mind.

"What else is troubling you?" I ask concerned.

"I know you don't want to hear the name, but I

have to talk to Mike about us immediately," he says softly.

"No, no, no! I don't know what he's going to say to you or what it will do to us. I'll talk to him."

"Fuck no! No, you hear me, no! You're not going near him. You're *mine!*" he says starkly and pulls at my hips.

"That's for sure," I roll my eyes and kiss him. "But what if he says something that makes you change your mind about us again?"

My hands are twisting on his chest. I just want to end this conversation and make love to him. But I sense he's not going to give up this crazy idea.

"That shit is over and done, Ellie. I'm not afraid of him or losing his friendship. I was scared your love for me wasn't as strong as what you once felt for him. That's in the past and buried, baby. I know we love each other in equal measure. My love for you is boundless. You and I were meant to be. We were written in the heavens, and there's nothing anyone could have done to keep us apart. You. Are. My. Life!"

Hearing him say that is my nirvana, my heaven on earth!

CHAPTER 42

I'm not convinced a conversation with Mike is the best idea right now.

We spend the next half hour going back and forth on why he should or shouldn't talk to Mike. When I offer to talk to Mike again, he immediately shuts me down.

I can stand up to Mike. Nothing he says will change my love for Jack.

Meeting Jack was a fortunate accident, and falling for each other was meant to be, but neither of us went looking for it. If I know Mike, and I know him well, he'll think I somehow concocted this entire thing just to piss him off, to get back at him.

Wouldn't that have been the sweetest revenge?

He would have deserved it, too.

He didn't see how devastated I was, how lost I was, and how I spent weekend after weekend in bed crying for him and feeling sorry for myself.

I had no expectations with Jack. How could I? I had nothing to offer. I was a mess of tortured emotions, a broken girl that no one could ever find remotely attractive. My joyful spirit was gone. Yet somehow, Jack saw something in me, and he stayed, and he cared, and he was there for me. I came back to life because of him.

If Mike disrupts that, he will answer to me!

For Jack's peace of mind, I accept his request, but he knows I'm worried.

"I hate that you feel you have to do this *now*. I will agree, but swear to me you don't have any reservations about us, and promise that no matter what he says, you'll come back to me," I beg.

He doesn't respond. He just smiles and moves me from his lap, gets out of bed, and puts on his jeans in a hurry.

He looks so damn yummy slipping on those jeans without his boxers. I'm gawking at him, imagining all the lustful, sexy things I want to do with him.

He's smirking, thoroughly enjoying that I'm drinking him in with my eyes.

"Marie!" he shouts, zipping up his jeans.

She's in my room in two seconds, eyes wide.

"Sup?" she asks, as she walks in.

"Grab that pink hair ribbon and come here, please," he points to the dresser.

I smile, because that's not a hair ribbon. It was wrapped around the Christmas present my mom sent me.

She glares at him, like he's lost his mind, but does as he asks.

Jack grabs me by the hips and pulls me, until I'm sitting at the edge of the bed.

He takes my hand, gets on one knee, and says...

"Be mine *forever after*, Ellie. Marry me!"

I'm stunned. I try to answer him, but my mouth is stuck open. I stare at him, astonished!

"Answer me, baby, please!"

I manage to nod yes, and he asks Marie to wrap the ribbon around our hands.

She moves quickly toward us and wraps it around our hands twice. It's loose and long, the excess falling to the floor.

I can't stop staring at him, but I sense Marie's jubilant smile for us.

"I'm yours, Ellie. I've been yours from the first time our lips touched. With this ribbon, I seal a promise I make to you right now to love you the rest of our lives. Nothing will ever keep us apart, ever. I *choose* you."

I squeal gleefully, throw myself at him, and knock him on his back to the floor. I'm on top of him kissing him, like a mad woman.

He's laughing, fully enjoying my assault.

"You're adorable," I say between kisses. "My Jack, my love, my everything," I kiss him again and again, until I see something move from the corner of my eye.

I look up for a second and see Marie is still here.

"Mhm, cray-cray," she giggles and walks out of the bedroom quietly clapping, thrilled for us.

Jack stands up and takes me with him. His arms are wrapped around my waist. My hands are around his back, my fingers digging into his muscles.

"I have to take care of this Mike thing right now," he squeezes me tighter. "I'll text you when it's done."

"Your iPhone's dead," I remind him.

"My work cell is in my car. It's an 818 number," he informs me. "But first, I need to love you one more time, because I think I missed a spot," he kisses my neck and pushes his erection into me.

"Yes you did, baby," I quickly unbutton his jeans.

స్టిస్టిస్టి

Jack left an hour ago, and I'm worried, very worried. I texted Sam as soon as Jack left and asked him to join him at Mike's place. He assured me he would, but I haven't heard from him either.

I'm anxiously pacing in the kitchen. I brought Marie up to speed, and she's trying to calm me down. Nothing she says makes me feel better.

I won't feel better until I hear from Jack.

One hour later, and I still haven't heard from Jack or Sam. I've taken a shower, put on my makeup, and styled my hair — I'm not sure why because I'm not going anywhere.

Still no news...

Marie is making lunch for me. I couldn't handle breakfast, and the four cups of coffee I've had are making me jittery.

She's sharing the latest news on Sam to distract me. It seems she's decided they're better off as friends.

I had been wondering what was going on with them, because as close as they are, the relationship didn't seem to be moving forward.

She has her sights set on a guy at work and thinks it can go somewhere. She had a conversation with Sam, and they agreed friendship is the best option.

I'm not entirely sure Sam feels the same way, but if Marie isn't into him, it's best they cut romantic ties now, when the friendship is intact and strong.

My iPhone pings, and I quickly check it.

818: It's done!

Ellie: Everything ok?

818: Yep

Ellie: Seriously?

818: Nothing that can't be fixed eventually

Ellie: Are YOU ok?

818: More than ok cause I have YOU!

Ellie: You're mine!

818: Always! I'll be there in an hour or so. I'm taking you somewhere

Ellie: Where?

818: You'll see. Sam is joining us

Ellie: Of course he is

818: LOL! He's texting Marie

Ellie: Where are we going? What should I wear?

818: Whatever you want

Ellie: My PJs?

818: Perfect

Ellie: Jack!

818: Ellie!

Ellie: What will YOU be wearing?

818: Black pants and a white shirt

Ellie: Tie?

818: No

Ellie: You're driving me nuts

818: I hope so!

Ellie: Yes please…Mmm over and over

818: You're fucking sexy!

Ellie: I want to eat you! Licking my lips

818: You're going to make me come

Ellie: Inside me

Why isn't he answering?

818: Sorry baby I'm running errands and people are eyeing me funny. You're fucking turning me on!

Ellie: Sorry!
818: LOL! Be ready in 1 hr
Ellie: Ok 😄 I love you!
Jack: I love you too my love!

CHAPTER 43

Whatever we're doing, wherever we're going, I want to look hot for Jack. I'm searching through my closet for something to wear, when I hear Marie behind me.

"Sam asked me to dress up."

"Dress up? Where are we going? Jack wouldn't tell me. Crap, I should dress up too."

I get back to the frantic hunt through my closet for something stunning to wear, when she chimes in with the perfect suggestion.

"Wear that fab hot-pink, short, strapless dress with the tulip skirt your mom sent you for Christmas. You still haven't worn it, and that color looks fantastic on you. I'll find it for you, but I need a favor. Remember those amazing strappy, black high heel shoes I wore last year? I need them, and I think they're in one of those boxes packed away in the garage. Will you go get them for me? Only because I can't reach those boxes, and you're taller," she begs, with an exaggerated batting of her eyelashes.

"But you have three other similar pairs in your closet. Can't you just wear one of those? You can wear my strappy, black ones." I'm hoping she'll let me off the hook.

Why is she sending me to the garage, when Jack will be here soon?

"One, your shoes are too big on me, and two, I want *those* strappy shoes, please." She gives me a playful, funny pout, and I can't refuse. She did bring Jack running over here with her little tricks. I owe her!

Fifteen minutes later, I have found the black shoes she wants and hand them to her. I head back to my room and find my hot-pink dress laid out on my bed, together with my brand new, ivory Vera Wang high heels, which I splurged on when my parents were still helping me pay my bills.

Marie has been rummaging through my closet, I can tell. This dress was in the spare room's closet, where we keep all our dressy outfits. I wonder what she was looking for. She must've borrowed something.

I get dressed and admire myself in the mirror,

feeling content now that Jack is on his way home to me.

Hmm, hot-pink does look great on me!

"They're here," Marie comes running into my room. She's got a wicked smile on her face, like she's hiding something.

Did she go out to greet them already?

I don't give it a second thought, because I'm too excited to see Jack.

I run outside.

Jack is standing next to a beautiful, brand new, silver metallic Mercedes Benz AMG S63 Cabriolet with red seats.

As stunning as the car is, all my attention is on him — *mmm, black pants and a white shirt never looked so hot on anyone!*

And the gratified grin on his face is the perfect accessory.

The top two buttons of his shirt are open. I'm aching to put my hands inside and touch him. His hair is naturally perfect, like always, and his bluish-gray eyes are checking me out from head to toe.

I'm going to explode!

"Hi, baby," he takes me by the hand and pulls me in for a kiss.

He smells fantastic. I don't know what cologne it is, but mixed with his own enticing scent — the biggest aphrodisiac of all — it's beyond mouth-watering!

Heaven help me!

I have to control my impure thoughts, because we won't be going anywhere if I don't.

"Whose car is this?" I ask.

"Rental, come," he replies confidently. He opens the convertible's door and guides me to the back seat, while Sam is grinning at us like he's got a huge secret.

"Why is Sam smiling like that? What are you guys up to?" I stare at each one of them.

Marie shrugs, like she's innocent of all charges. If she had any idea, she would tell me.

"No idea, baby," replies Jack and sits next to me. He puts the seat belt around me, fastens his, and then takes my hand and kisses it.

Damn, I could take him right now!

ಌಌಌ

Marie is clearly in charge of the music on our ride to who-knows-where. We're listening to an assortment of songs, from Justin Timberlake's "Mirrors" to Rihanna's "Diamonds" and Maroon 5's "Sugar." She's keeping us entertained during this surprise adventure.

Sam's driving and trying, in vain, to pick music he likes. Marie quickly slaps his hand away from touching her iPhone.

Ariana Grande is up with "Into You." Marie and

I are loudly singing, very much off-key, while we dance to the beat in our seats.

I turn to Jack, point at him, and trace his lips with my fingers, while I sing. He's grinning, enjoying my display and my fingers on his lips. He catches one of them and bites down.

"Ouch," I mouth but keep singing.

The beat of Sentidos Opuestos' "Eternamente" is starting to blare, when Jack taps Marie on the shoulder and asks her to turn the volume down.

She ruefully complies.

He leers at me, and I have the urge to jump him, but first I need to know where we're going.

"Vegas," he says, with a clever smile.

"Vegas, for the weekend?" I ask excited.

"So I can marry you," his tone is cool and serene.

"Marry me!" I practically shout back.

"You don't want to marry me?" he pouts playfully.

Sam and Marie are chuckling listening to us.

"Did you know about this?" I stare straight at Marie.

"Nope," she giggles, from the front seat.

I narrow my eyes at Sam, because he knew, for sure he was in on this entire scheme.

"Mrs. Milian, answer me," he prods.

Geez, I love the sound of that!

"Do you or don't you want to marry me as, soon as we get to Vegas?" He's grinning splendidly.

I stare at him for a second. I unbuckle my seat

belt and straddle him. I wrap my arms around his neck, lean in, and whisper in his ear, "It will be my pleasure and a privilege to love you and wake up next to you the rest of my life, baby." I look at him in love and kiss him softly.

"No, baby, the pleasure and privilege are all mine," he immediately answers and kisses me back.

"I need that answer so everyone here can hear you, Mrs. Milian," he's examining me, overjoyed that I said yes. His hands are on my behind, his fingers digging into me.

I stare at him for a second, smiling blissfully, and say, "Mrs. Valencia *hyphen* Milian would *love* to marry you, as soon as we get to Vegas."

"Oh, baby, as long as you're mine, I'll call you whatever you want, Mrs. Valencia *hyphen* Milian," he teases.

Marie jumps up and down in her seat, "Yay, love wins!"

I look up at the beautiful sky, the warm air playing with my hair, and throw my arms up.

Jack's face is pressed against my chest, and his arms are wrapped tightly around me.

How did this happen?

How did we find each other?

Thank you, universe, for working your magic!

Thank you!

I look down at him, and we stare at each other.

I kiss him and mouth on his lips, "My Jack."

"Forever after, baby," he responds.

CHAPTER 44

We arrive at the Aria hotel and leave the car with the valet. I'm blissfully in my own personal piece of heaven with Jack.

He's going to be my husband soon!

We're holding hands, as we walk through the lobby to the front desk and check in.

"What time did you book the chapel, and where is it?" Jack asks Sam.

"We have an hour, and it's in the hotel," replies Sam, after checking the time on his cell. "You're going to love it, I promise."

"We have forty-five minutes to freshen up, and we'll meet back here at a quarter to," says Jack.

We all head to the elevators.

Our suite is fantastic. It's huge and overlooks

the strip. There are ten or twelve enormous bouquets of white roses and calla lilies all over the rooms, and there's a bottle of Champaign chilling on the center table in the sitting room, with a tray of chocolate covered strawberries next to it. The bathroom is also incredible, with a massive tub.

Mmm, we're sure going to enjoy that amenity!
My baby went all out.

This suite must have cost him a pretty penny. I have no idea how much or if he can afford it. I hope he's not overspending on me. I'm happy with just that immense bed, as long as he's in it with me.

"Well, Mrs. Valencia-Milian, we have about thirty minutes. What should we do?"

"What do you want to do, Mr. Milian?" I give him a libidinous look.

"Hmm, well I think we both want to christen that bed," he pulls my hips into his erection.

"I think I want to wait on the bed," I reply mischievously.

He narrows his eyes, wondering where I'm going with this.

I eye the huge desk, lick my lower lip, and grin.

"The desk?" he asks amused.

"The desk, the sofa, the chair," I giggle.

He's my husband — *well, legally he will be in half an hour*. I shouldn't be coy around him.

"Your wish is my command, baby. Dress on or

off?"

"On, as long as you handle it carefully. I'm going to marry a very handsome man in thirty minutes, and it has to be pristine," I wink at him.

"Lucky him," he walks me to the desk, while kissing me.

When he's got me pinned against it, he reaches under my dress and pulls down my panties.

"Up," he orders, referring to my feet, so he can remove my lacy undies. "Beautiful," he observes and places them on the bed.

He walks to the bathroom and comes back with a few towels. "I don't want you to get a rash on your beautiful *bum*," he spreads a towel on the desk.

I gaze at him, smiling, lusting for him, my gorgeous, endearing, hot husband. I want to take him now, but I let him finish what he's doing, because he's intent on taking care of me, and I love him for it.

He helps me up on the desk, making sure I'm not sitting on any part of the dress, and stands between my legs. Then he begins to unzip it.

"Dress on," I remind him

"I know, baby, but I'm just undoing it a bit, because I need skin-to-skin access to these," he grabs my breasts.

My hot boob man!

"Done?" I giggle, looking at his adorable face.

He nods yes.

"My turn," I bite my lip in anticipation. I unbutton his shirt and pants, pull down the zipper, and open them. But I don't push them down to remove them.

"I'm keeping these on?" he asks with mirth.

I nod yes, kiss him, and grab his erection.

He's ready, very ready.

He pulls the top of my dress down, so he can stroke my breasts. "I love your soft skin, baby," he says, as he's caressing me.

I pull him closer to me by his shirt, and he smiles. "I need you inside me," I mumble on his lips.

"Mmm, yes, baby," he answers and enters me slowly. I moan, enjoying the feel of him inside me. He stays there not moving.

"This is where I want you, like this, inside me, always," I whisper in his ear.

"Mmm, my favorite place to be," he replies.

I'm enthralled by the feel of him, the exquisite, satisfying, ecstasy inside me. His hands are pulling me into him firmly. My arms are laced around his neck, my legs around his hips. His lips are on mine, his tongue claiming me.

"Fast and hard, please, Jack," I beg on his lips.

"Okay, hold on tight, baby," he warns and complies. He starts to move, fast, rough, hard, pounding.

"Ahh, don't stop, baby. I love you!" I moan,

savoring his every move.

My head is nestled in the apex of his neck, and I'm sucking and biting it. But I quickly move to a spot near his shoulder. I don't want him walking down the aisle with a hickey on his neck.

His hands pull at my hips, and he's thrusting harder and deeper inside me, again and again. He's working me hard, and it's delicious, exhilarating, and powerful.

He's mine, all mine. I can take him any time I want. I can love him as often as I want. I'm lost in the pleasure gushing through my body. I bite down on him, and he groans.

He thrusts into me again harder and deeper.

"My Ellie. My love. My wife," he grunts against my neck, as he's thrusting harder, and his hands are digging into my hips through my dress.

"Yes, baby. I love you!" I moan, biting down on him with every hard and deep thrust.

"Ahh, Jack!" I cry out.

"Ellie!" he moans, and we both come, exhausted and sated.

"That was quite satisfying, baby, thank you," he grins wickedly at me and kisses my forehead. "I like the way you think," he slowly pulls out of me.

"I like the way you fuck," I sass with a shameless grin. "There will be plenty of times when quickies will be on the menu, dear *husband*. I hope you can comply," I kiss him. I take his lower lip and pull at it with my lips and tongue.

"Mmm," he moans and then opens his eyes. "Oh, I can comply, Mrs. Valencia-Milian," he's staring me down suggestively.

"Hmm, I think I prefer just Mrs. Milian," I assert happily, zip up his pants, and button his shirt.

He doesn't reply.

He takes the panties from the bed, puts them over my shoes, and pulls them up to my knees. He helps me down from the desk and pulls the lacy undies all the way up. He zips up my dress, hugs me, and kisses my hair.

"You are my everything, Ellie. I love you."

"I love you too, Jack," I reply adoringly.

He walks me to the sofa. I sit on his lap with my arms around his neck, my hands playing with his hair, and my head resting on his shoulder.

"Does it hurt?" I touch the spot where I bit him.

"Not enough to complain. The harder you bite, the better job I'm doing. Bite all you want, baby," he says pleased with himself, making me giggle.

"I should make reservations for us to have dinner after the wedding and maybe go out to celebrate. Where do you want to go?" he asks suddenly and shifts around, searching for his iPhone.

I don't want him to move. I want to stay like this, snuggled on his lap.

"Let's just go to a buffet," I grin against his neck and kiss him. "I hear the one at Caesars Palace is spectacular."

"Seriously?" he's surprised.

"Sure."

"You're unexpected, Ellie, just another reason I love you so much," he kisses my hair.

"It's just food, and the buffet has lots of it. Marie and Sam can party on, if they want. I would rather you bring me back here so we can make good use of that massive bed and that tub," I leer up at him.

"Whatever you want, baby."

"I should call Rob. He won't forgive me, if I don't make him part of this wedding," I suddenly realize my bestie can't miss this significant day.

"I already called him," he informs me.

I look up at him, grinning.

Of course he did. My thoughtful husband!

He kisses me lightly on the tip of my nose. "I'll ask Marie to FaceTime him at the wedding. She packed a bag for you, by the way. We'll pick it up from her room later."

"Thank you, baby," I bury my face in the nape of his neck again and take in his scent. That sensual, delicious Jack scent I'll be waking up to the rest of my life.

"You know, our parents are probably going to kill us for eloping," I say, nibbling gently at his neck.

"Yea, probably," he agrees between moans, as our hands are intertwined, our fingers playfully twisting.

"We can have another wedding. Would you like that?" he offers.

"Would you?"

"If it would make them happy and if you want to, of course."

"Would it make you happy?" I look up and gaze into his eyes.

"Ellie, I'd marry you again every year, easily."

I smile at him and kiss him on the corner of his lips.

"I suppose another wedding would be okay. It will certainly make the talking-to we're going to get a lot easier."

"That's for sure," he chuckles. "What kind of wedding do you want, large or small?"

"Small, I think. Just close friends and family, at the beach or a vineyard, maybe. Catalina Island would be nice, if it's not too expensive."

I'm examining him, playing with his hair, tracing his lips, touching his face.

My Jack, my husband.

"Don't worry about the cost, baby. I will always take care of you."

"I'm sure you will, Jack, but I don't want us spending money we don't have. I mean, don't get me wrong, I can spend money. But now that we're going to be family, I have to be more careful and so do you."

"I make enough money, baby," he assures me and caresses my cheek.

"I don't know what you make, and I'm not asking you to disclose your finances right now. I just want us to be financially responsible. And...I can't believe that statement just came out of my mouth," I laugh.

"I don't only manage the chain of coffee shops, Ellie, I own a majority stake. My company — *our company*, Milian Ventures & Investments — not only owns JP Cafetería but has other investments, and it's doing exceptionally well. We're not multi-millionaires yet, but we're well on our way. Believe me. We're in a great place financially."

I look at him incredulous. Not because I don't believe him, but because this is all news to me.

He owns his own company?

"Well, aren't you a catch, lucky the bitch that nabs you!" I tease.

He laughs openly. "Yes, she is," he kisses me. "So, about that wedding..." he continues.

"Still small," I rest my head on his shoulder again. "Catalina would be nice. I want something cozy, intimate, and fun all at the same time. It should be a celebration of our love. I'd like people to enjoy themselves, like a big, fun party. Of course we'll have a priest marry us, bless our union, but after that, it should be party. I don't want any snobbery, people snickering about the chicken or fish, or if the flowers are up to their expectations. We'll give them tacos, and they'll like it," I giggle and he laughs. "It should just be a fun celebration, like the wedding scene in the movie Mamma Mia! Remember?"

"Never seen it," he scoffs.

Of course he's never seen it...We'll have to rent it, and I'm positive he'll watch it just to please me.

"Well, like that, pure fun."

"How soon do you want to do it?"

"I don't know. I'm in no hurry. We're going to be married like in ten minutes, so it's a done deal. Six months, a year, two years," I shrug.

"Six months, at the most," he says. "I want to share that moment with you as soon as possible."

"Okay, six months at the most," I kiss him.

CHAPTER 45

Jack and I are in the elevator holding hands, heading down to the lobby to meet Sam and Marie.

He looks pensive

Something's on his mind.

"What is it, baby?" I look up at him adoringly.

"Will it be Mrs. Valencia-Milian or..." he trails off. "I'm okay with either," he promises.

I know which would make him happier, and the truth is I'd be delighted to take on his last name.

"Mrs. Milian," I confirm elated and completely sure of my decision.

He nods okay, smiling broadly.

"Oh, by the way, Mrs. Milian," he pulls me into a tight embrace. "I don't have a diamond ring for you. I want you to choose it. I want to see your eyes light up, when you find the perfect one."

I reach up and kiss him softly on the lips.

"*You* are the light in my eyes, Jack, but thank you. We'll choose the perfect one together."

He kisses me back, "Okay, let's go get hitched!"

࿂࿂࿂

The chapel is beautiful, exactly what I would've chosen had I been in charge of the planning. It's chic, refined, with neutral tones and romantic lighting. The aisle is adorned with big bouquets of white roses and calla lilies.

Just like our suite.

It's simple, elegant, and breathtaking.

"You did this?" I gaze at him completely in love.

"Sam," he confesses.

I turn to Sam, who is standing behind us, and hug him.

"Congratulations," he says sweetly.

"Thank you!"

I'm thanking him for chasing after Marie and bringing Jack as his wing man.

I'm thanking him for supporting me — even reluctantly — when I went to confront Mike.

I'm thanking him for having our back, when he found out Jack and I were seeing each other, and for having Jack's back, when he talked to Mike.

I'm basically thanking him for bringing Jack to me.

The officiant is waiting for us. It's time to walk down the aisle, but Marie won't let us, until she's taken enough photos and videos of Jack and I entering, kissing, gazing into each other's eyes. Take after take to document this day for our friends and family, she insists.

She's done ten minutes later, when Jack kindly makes her stop.

"Marie, I'd really like to marry my baby now, please," he gives her an enough-is-enough grin, and she concedes.

We're standing at the entrance of the chapel, where Marie placed us just seconds ago, so Rob can see every detail through FaceTime.

We're embracing, gazing into each other's eyes.

"Are you ready to marry me?" he pulls me in tighter.

"Yes," I look at him enamored.

"I'm going to be yours in a second, Ellie, and you'll be mine forever after," he's lovingly gazing into my eyes, holding me tightly.

"I'm already yours, Jack, forever. I was yours even before we met. You have my heart," I kiss him tenderly on the lips.

He kisses me back and whispers,

"You *Are* My Heart."

EPILOGUE

The Vows

Jack

Ellie, I love you. I took a few detours after finding you, but I know that any road I could have ever taken would have ultimately led me back to you. You are my light, my reason, my sanity, my motivation, my love. In a thousand years, I'll still be in love with you, adoring you, appreciating you, craving you. I will support you, take care of you, and treasure you for the rest of your life. My heart is open, wide open for you. I am completely yours. Thank you for fighting for me, for not giving up on me, for loving me, for choosing me. I choose you too, Ellie Isabel Valencia, my everything, my wife, my Mrs. Milian.

Ellie

Jack, I love you. I loved you even before we met. I was put on this earth for you, because in the midst of darkness, it was you I found. You are my rock, my love, my reason, my genie-in-a-bottle wish come true. I love every single part of you, inside and out. I love your kindness, your heart, your sincerity, your spontaneity, the way you look at me, the way you love me. I love that you took me to the top of the mountain, literally and figuratively. You are my heart, my soul, my happiness. You are my everything, my truest love now and forever. I choose you too. Thank you for seeing me, for loving me, my husband, my love, my Jack.

THE "TALK"

Jack, Mike, and Sam

Sam: I'm meeting you at Mike's
Jack: What? Who told you?
Sam: Who'd you think? Ellie's worried
Jack: It'll be fine
Sam: I know. I'll just stay outside in case he throws
    you out the window
Jack: Fuck you!
Sam: Ok asshole

✿✿✿

I'm already outside Mike's apartment, when Jack arrives. I have to keep these two fools from killing each other, so Ellie doesn't end up without a boyfriend.

Shit, and to think I'm partially responsible for their hook up. I would've never guessed they'd end up together.

Jack looks annoyed that I'm here and gives me a "hey" tilt of the head, as he walks toward Mike's apartment.

Fuck, I told him I'd stay outside, but fuck it!

"Hey, man, come in," Mike welcomes Jack and

leaves the door open.

Before Jack can close the door, I hold it and walk in behind him. He turns to me and sneers.

"What's up, Sam," Mike greets me. He doesn't see anything odd that I'm here too.

"Grab some beers from the fridge," Mike says.

I take the hint and head to the kitchen. I can already feel the tension building up, as Jack prepares to confront Mike.

Mike sits on the sofa to continue watching the soccer game on TV. Jack sits on the armrest.

I grab the beers from the fridge, close the door, and lean against it. I figure from here it'll take me seconds to get to them, if they come to blows.

I'm so fucking grateful this studio is so small.

"I need to talk to you," Jack begins.

"About what?" Mike replies, distracted by the game.

"Ellie," Jack's tone is serious.

Mike turns to Jack frowning, looks at me, then back to Jack. "Why's he here?"

"To keep the peace," I reply and place the beers on a small table near the fridge.

"So talk," Mike turns to Jack, his expression hardened. He rolls his eyes and then looks back at the TV. He knows he's not going to like what Jack has to say.

"I love her, and she loves me," Jack says bluntly.

Mike's gaze remains on the game.

"Beer," orders Mike and stretches his arm toward me.

I hand it to him, give Jack his, and step back to the fridge. Jack's looking at his beer, waiting for Mike to respond.

"How do you know," Mike questions Jack, "that she loves you?"

"Come on, man. You want details?" Jack stares at him.

"Fuck yea, I want details. One day she's in love with me and the next, you *think* she loves *you*?" Mike's tone is critical and recriminating.

"I don't *think*," Jack answers calmly but forcefully, "I know!"

"What the fuck, Jack. How the fuck..."

"It's kind of my fault," I interrupt. "I forced them to interact, because I needed a wing man. Marie wouldn't go out otherwise."

"Fuck you, Sam. Stay out of this. He's the fucking traitor," Mike points angrily at Jack with his beer. "It's his fault!"

"It's *your* fault, Mike," Jack eyeballs him, "and frankly, I'm grateful."

"Grateful, motherfucker!" Mike shouts at Jack and stands up, staring him down.

"Yea, grateful, because I love her," Jack replies vehemently. "And it *is* your fault. Don't forget we know what you did to her, how you treated her. We were there every time you walked away, every time you made her feel like shit. You discarded her!"

"So you saw an opening and pounced on her, piece of shit!" Mike counters angrily.

"Fuck you, man! That's not what happened." Jack is shouting back at him.

"How did it happen? Fuck, Jack, there are thousands of women in this city. Why her?" Mike sneers, pissed.

"We didn't plan it. It just happened," Jack replies more calmly.

"Nothing just fucking happens, asshole!"

"I told you how it happened," I interrupt Mike.

"Fine, Sam," he stares me down. "But Jack didn't have to move in on her," he points at him, his fuming eyes burning into Jack.

"She's special. I fell for her," says Jack.

"I know she's special, thank you! I was with her for three fucking years," Mike scoffs.

"Then why'd you let her go?" Jack questions him, knowing he won't have an answer, not one that makes any sense.

Mike paces around, his anger and frustration boiling over. He can't come up with a rational answer.

"Fuck you. She loves *me*! I've told you that a million times. I told you she'd *always* be mine, and I can get her back whenever *I* want!"

"You did say that," Jack says evenly, "and I believed you and almost lost her. We love each other. Those are the facts right now."

"Have you fucked her?" Mike scowls.

"Fuck you, asshole!" Jack stands up livid.

"I was her first. Did you know that? She chose me. You can never have that!" Mike's words reek of poisonous scorn.

Jack closes his eyes for a second, as in pain from Mike's vile jab, but he's just trying to control his anger. When he opens them, he's reined it in enough to respond.

"I'll be her last," he says calmly. He knows Mike's just trying to push him to his breaking point. But Ellie is his, *only* his, and that's a fact. "And that's what matters."

"Son of a bitch!" Mike swings at Jack, but Jack deflects the fist that's heading straight for his jaw.

I jump between them and hold Jack back from returning the punch and ending him — Jack can take him and two more at the same time.

"Stop, you fucking morons!" I scream at them. "You're fucking friends, assholes. Remember that!"

"Fuck you, Sam. This *is your* fault!" Mike hisses at me.

"Fuck you, Mike! It's about fucking time *you* take responsibility for your own fuck ups!" I'm in his face, pointing at him. "You fucked up and lost. Deal with that shit!"

I step away and look from one to the other. "We've been friends since we were kids. Can't you work this shit out?"

"Not going to happen today," Mike says with a disdainful tone, sits on the sofa, and stares at the game.

"I'll always consider you my friend, Mike, but I love her, and I'm not letting her go. I thought I owed it to you to tell you in person," says Jack steadily.

Mike takes a long drink of his beer, ignoring him.

Jack knows this conversation is over, places his bottle of beer on the floor and leaves. I follow him and close the door behind me.

"Fuck! Now what?" I say, rattled by what just happened.

We're walking toward the cars to leave, when he abruptly stops.

"Now I marry her," he says, as if that's the logical answer to my rhetorical question.

"What the fuck! Did he hit you on the head, when I wasn't looking?"

"Fuck off! Are you going help me or not?" he responds.

"Help you? Fucker, this isn't something you can decide on your own. How do you know she even wants to marry you?"

"I asked her this morning, and she said yes." He's grinning from ear to ear, like he just had an epiphany.

"Ooookay. So, when's the wedding?" I ask stupefied, because he's insane.

"Today," he responds with total certainty.

"What the fuck, Jack! It's settled, you won, she's yours. You don't have to rush into anything!"

"I'm not rushing. I just know." He's still grinning like the idiot he is.

"So, how is this going to happen today exactly?" There's no way they can get married on a Saturday afternoon in LA.

"Vegas, I'm going to surprise her."

"You're out of your fucking mind, Jack! What if she doesn't want to marry you today?" He's not making any sense, the fool.

"Then we'll just have a helluva weekend in Vegas."

"Are you sure?"

"Yea, man, if she's not up for marrying me today, I know we'll get married soon, though I'm hoping for today. Are you in or not?"

"Of course, you romantic son of a bitch," I smirk.

"Fuck you!" He stares me down grinning. "Just make reservations for us at the Aria, Bellagio or something similar. A big suite for us, and ask them to fill it with flowers, white roses to start. And of course rooms for you and Marie, unless it's just one room for you guys..." he trails off.

I shake my head no. "We're a better match as

friends."

"Okay, here's my card. And book a chapel too, a nice one. I mean it, Sam. I don't want Elvis marrying us," he demands.

"No Elvis, check. And what will *you* be doing while I'm working my fingers to the bone?"

"My assistant, Georgia, will help you with the documents for the marriage license," he's texting her as he speaks. "Drop me off at a car rental in Beverly Hills," he continues ordering, like a fucking drill sergeant.

I frown at him confused — *he has a car, I have a car...*

"I'm going to rent a convertible," he explains. "I'll leave mine at your place, rent the convertible, and then I'll get the rings at Tiffany."

"Tiffany! Do you have any idea what a diamond costs at Tiffany? Fucker, how much money do you make?" I ask dumfounded.

"I'm just getting the wedding bands. I'll get the diamond later, let her choose one she likes," he replies, laughing at me.

"Text Marie, and tell her we're headed to Vegas. Ask her to pack a bag for Ellie but without her knowing, because it's a surprise. Do not tell her that my intention is to marry Ellie, because that secret she will definitely not be able to keep to herself. And ask her to dress up. I'll text Ellie."

"Anything else, Mr. Milian, Sir?" I roll my eyes.

"Yea, make sure you shower and put on dress pants and a shirt, no jeans," he orders.

Shower! What are you, my mother, you fucking bossy SOB! If you weren't my best friend, I'd kick your ass!

"What?" he asks, like he can hear my irreverent thoughts.

"Nothing."

"We'll meet back at Ellie's in an hour or so. I'll text you when I'm on my way," he starts walking to his car.

I drop him off at the rental and head back home. I text Marie, before I start working on complying with *His Majesty's* requests.

Sam: Need a favor
Marie: What
Sam: You can't tell Ellie
Marie: Why?
Sam: It's a surprise from Jack
Sam: He's taking her to Vegas today
Marie: Ok
Sam: We're going too
Marie: Well that's a surprise!
Sam: Prepare a bag for her don't let her see you
Marie: Ok. Anything else?
Sam: Dress up like in a nice dress heels or
    something
Marie: Why?
Sam: It's a surprise
Marie: Tell me
Sam: Just do it please. Surprise!
Marie: Fine

I make reservations at the Aria, a suite for them and rooms for Marie and me, plus the chapel, which I pay for — my wedding gift to them.

Shit, I hope she marries him, because I won't get a refund.

We arrive at Marie's at the same time. Jack's in a brand new, silver metallic Mercedes Benz AMG S63 Cabriolet with red interior.

I'm convinced he's been holding out on me, and his company is doing a hell of a lot better than I thought.

Fucker, and he just turned 26!

I eye the car with envy, and he throws me the keys.

"You're driving," he smirks. "My future wife and I have business to discuss in the back seat," he winks, proud of himself.

Sly, romantic motherfucker!

TRANSLATIONS

Muñeca (muñe): Doll — In Spanish, it's used as a term of endearment i.e. sweetie.

¡Salud!: Cheers!

Las Mañanitas: A traditional Mexican song, accompanied by mariachi, that's sung to people on their birthday.

Michelada: Your favorite chilled Mexican beer — highly recommend: Dos XX Lager, Corona, Pacífico — mixed with a ¼ cup (more or less) of lime or lemon juice and salt to your liking. Some people opt to add tomato juice and/or hot sauce. As for the hot sauce, I'd recommend Tapatio or Valentina.

ABOUT THE AUTHOR

J M RAPHAELLE

♥ Mexican-American
😊 Bilingual
🏫 BA, Columbia College Chicago
🏡 Lives in Southern California

Instagram: JMRaphaelle
Twitter: J_M_Raphaelle
FB: JMRaphaelleAuthor & AuthorJMR
www.JMRaphaelle.com

THE THING ABOUT EVER AFTER...

BOOK 2 OF THE TRILOGY

For more information, visit:
www.JMRaphaelle.com

THE THING ABOUT LOVE...©

A NOVEL BY

J M RAPHAELLE

Made in the USA
Middletown, DE
11 June 2023